W9-CJF-652

THE SECOND LIFE
OF

CAPTAIN
CONTRERAS

BY

TORCUATO LUCA DE TENA

translated and edited
by
Barnaby Conrad

HOUGHTON MIFFLIN COMPANY BOSTON

The Riverside Press Cambridge

1960

c. 2

First Printing

HR
NOV 15 '60

THE SECOND LIFE OF

CAPTAIN CONTRERAS

THE SECOND LIFE OF

CAPTAIN CONTRERAS

PREFACE

The first signs of life, according to the best calculation, must have been at seven-twenty in the morning of that September 5th, 1950, when the remains of Captain Contreras were being moved from the old abandoned Santo Tomé parish in Toledo to a new resting place in the Almudena Cemetery. It is *not* true that he opened his own coffin lid himself, nor that he rapped on the inside to get the attention of the gravediggers. And it is, of course, completely ridiculous that he suddenly jumped from the truck, as reported by the *New York Mirror,* "causing terror among the stunned passers-by until he was subdued by three armed policemen!"

The irresponsibility on the part of the press in general in the case of Captain Contreras was incredible and often shameful. The traffickers in sensationalism had a field day, with little regard for such trivia as the real facts. Now that several years have passed since the event and the air of hysteria which surrounded the reappearance of Contreras has calmed down, the time has come to set the record straight.

First of all, virtually everything we know about Alonso Contreras' life in the sixteenth and seventeenth centuries we owe to his own sketchy and unfinished Memoirs, which he apparently wrote at the request of the great Lope de Vega. These memoirs (discovered by Serrano y Sanz and published first in the *Bulletin of the Academy of History* in 1900)* throw some light on the personality of the man, but in general are disappointing and don't help us much when it comes to the modern Contreras who made his appearance several centuries after those writings were finished.

To return to the story, which will be reconstructed in this preface around the basic facts that are known to us: Alonso Contreras' coffin was rather well preserved, being constructed of iron. It, along with the remains of several other citizens of the sixteenth and seventeenth centuries, was to be removed from the partially flooded crypts in the cellar of the condemned building.

The move took place at dawn. The living members of that journey of the dead, by a strange and very Spanish reaction, felt they should make macabre jokes, and so they hummed such doleful ditties as:

> *With the tibia bone and the fibula bone*
> *The boys will make lovely skates . . .*

* Afterwards reprinted in the *Revista de Occidente* with a masterly and anonymous prologue whose style clearly belonged to one of the most delightful prose writers of our contemporary literature.

However, when Alonso's casket was finally opened in the cemetery, every irreverent jest gagged and rattled in the throat of even the jolliest gravedigger.

What silenced them was not only the surprise of finding the bulk of a body where they expected to find a mound of dust or at most a heap of rotting bones; nor was it the sight of the moldered shroud covering that bulk which gave it a phantasmal look. Nor was it the size, nor the smell. It was the movement: the slow, barely perceptible rhythmic rise of its chest. I don't want to linger here on what is well known to everyone. The terror of the gravediggers has been described both then and now by writers more adept than I at dramatizing a scene.

The episodes following the discovery are also known: The notice to the Supervisor of Burial Grounds; the moving of the body to the morgue, and the chilling removal of the putrefied bandages by a medical student. Scissors were unnecessary. The shroud fell apart in his fingers like burnt paper. Underneath was the naked body of a man. It was covered with a heavy layer of a greasy substance. The breast rose and fell and the faint heartbeats were frighteningly rapid. What caused the most revulsion — more than the pale violet color, more than the stink of the greasy scaly limbs — was the wild beard that fell to his waist, giving a monstrous distortion to his face. And the claws — the extended nails which elongated the length of his hands and feet grotesquely.

Then came the notice to the police; the hurricane effect of the news in Madrid; the timidity of the Spanish press in deciding to admit an event already made known throughout the world by the exuberant imagination of foreign correspondents . . .

The Chief of General Security roundly refused to make any statement on the case; from the pulpits the faithful were reminded of their stern obligation not to spread or believe in that "sorcery" till science or the Church itself should make a statement on the event.

The still breathing body of Contreras was installed, after the first day, in the Municipal Hospital of San Juan de Dios. Dr. Salvador Yuste took charge of it. They cleaned the body under his direction, cropped the beard and long locks of hair, cut his nails and for five days watched, minute by minute, the reactions of the patient. In the meantime the chemical laboratory of the Police Department analyzed the remains of the shroud, the nail cuttings, the grease and the beard.

At twelve minutes past one of the sixth day, with Dr. Yuste himself on duty in the room, the breathing of the resurrected man became deeper and slower.

"Jesús!" came from his lips.

The fingers of his right hand moved as though trying to undo a strong invisible binding.

The doctor went up to him, gently lifted his eyelids and placed the tremulous light of a match near his dry pupils. He could not help feeling uneasy before those owl-eyes which looked out at him unseeingly.

Dr. Salvador Yuste, an enigmatic figure, was at that time forty-eight years old. About all we know of him is that his father had been a smuggler in the Valley of Arán, his mother a laundress in Irun, and by smuggling French perfumes and liquor his parents were able to afford his first schooling. But Salvador had dreams of bettering himself, so he went to college, determined to carve out a great career for himself. He alternated his studies with his job at the railway station where he carried suitcases to pay his tuition. And his father helped until he was killed by the police. Perhaps because of his spotty schooling and humble beginnings, Yuste had not gone as far in the medical world as his gnawing ambition demanded. He was a very ambitious man — not necessarily for money, but for recognition.

It was still night. Dr. Yuste approached the man with the beard again and took his pulse. Upon touching him he thought he noticed a faint light movement beneath his skin as though the resurrected man had felt the contact of the doctor's hand. Then he opened his lips and moved them as though wishing to speak, but no sound came from his mouth. Yuste brought up a chair and studied him hard, watching for any possible reaction. Who would this man turn out to be? What tragedy or what madness had driven him to this sham? To Salvador Yuste there was no doubt: this person had meticulously prepared his stunt with incredible audacity and no small knowledge of medicine. The man was undoubtedly a lunatic to have had himself buried alive, in exchange for . . . in exchange for what? For cheap fame, perhaps? Publicity?

The faint germ of a scheme began to take form in Yuste's brain . . . faint, faint as a glowworm's lamp . . .

The doctor kept staring at the resuscitated man, but with a new interest. Without taking his eyes off him, he removed his spectacles and began to clean the lenses with his handkerchief. He gave a brief laugh.

"Impossible . . . Madness! But . . ." And he squirmed in his seat, intrigued by the struggle beginning to unfold inside of him. "If I knew how . . . If I dared . . ."

But the director of the hospital had already issued a statement on the case. "After the hospital," he had said, jerking his head toward the subject, "either jail or the insane asylum!"

Yuste clamped his rimless spectacles onto his sweaty nose. Was Dr. Lafuente's opinion beyond questioning? The morbid and romantic imagination of the public would want to believe whoever defended the possibility of resurrection, after who knows how many years of sleep, rather than the arguments of those who wanted to expose a humbug. The secret of any success lay in boldness, in knowing the exact time to make one's move, to take advantage of a rare opportunity.

Válame la Virgen!" suddenly cried a voice. "Confession!"

A tickling of fear rose like a swarm of ants to Yuste's temples and his pounding heart seemed to want to escape from his breast. There was no doubt about it. The man with the beard was sitting up in the bed watching him intently. His lips were moving as though trying to speak, and his convulsive breathing shook his cadaverous shoulders. He stayed like that a few seconds.

"To wash my honor clean," he gasped finally. "Or sup with Christ!"

Pause. His breathing resounded like a bellows. Then he fell back on the bed and went into a trance again.

Dr. Yuste, nailed to his chair, without moving a muscle of his face, stayed watching his patient for a long time. Finally he removed his spectacles mechanically, took out a handkerchief and with trembling fingers began to clean the lenses once more.

II

Now let us go back in time — far back to the year 1633 — to an important day; we must go back that far if we are to link this incredible tale with the present.

The late afternoon was brown and gold. The setting sun splashed the great Toledo plain and a golden rain seemed to gild the empty fields and canyons. Even the waters of the Tagus sparkled with restless little mirrors which caught the sun's last rays.

Alonso de Contreras was sitting on the ground in a ravine. His bearded chin rested on his hands, his hands rested on his sword hilt, and the sword rested between his legs like a cane. He was thinking. A group of naked little boys shouted and played in the Tagus. There were some women, obviously of Moorish descent, carrying enormous baskets on their heads; others with water buckets leaning against one hip held out the opposite arm for balance; a boastful young cavalier, twirling his mustache, flirted with them as they went by.

Alonso watched them pass. His beard was more silver than he would have wished. The deep circles under his eyes gave him a dark look of melancholy which did not detract from the strength of his features or the hard brilliance of his eyes. Many incidents of his turbulent and roving life were marching across the stage of his memories. Alonso had never been a meditative man. Past and future had never existed for him. Prototype of the man of action, the moment at hand was what had always completely absorbed him.

In all his life Alonso de Contreras had only twice found himself at crossroads where, deprived of action, he had resorted to thought. He was such an extremist that on the first occasion he had become a monk and on the second he had written his memoirs. In a man of his character the simple act of taking parchment and scratching on it with a goose quill to write his memoirs turned out to be the hardest adventure of his life. Alonso de Contreras plunged into the adventure of thought with the same attitude that he used in boarding a ship under enemy fire in his pirate days against the Turks. The difference was that in the latter case others as crazy as he followed him, while in the adventure of the memoirs he plunged alone.

Sitting on the ground in the ravine, Alonso de Contreras kept thinking. He was thinking of the thousand exploits which had led him, a powerful governor and redoubtable captain, to Toledo pursued by the law where each tree shadow might be a hangman.

Alonso's mind leapt back to his youth — back to when he was the young Lieutenant Contreras in the company commanded by Pedro Xaraba del Castillo. The company was in Hornacho, a place swarming with Moors. Alonso was then only twenty-two years old, but he had already spent nine years as a pirate in the Mediterranean. One ill-fated day he happened to discover a cache of Moorish arms. He reported his discovery to the Commissar only. No one else. This incident influenced the course of his life so much that from then on Contreras became a plaything of fate. Commissar Osorio never transmitted Contreras' report. When after five years the Moorish plot was discovered and it was known that Contreras knew of the arms, he was accused of being mixed up in the ugly business.

Alonso left his company because of his Captain's jealousy. The Captain was a dainty fop who wanted to sleep with Isabel Rojas, who was Contreras' sweetheart and pregnant by him.

"Sir," a soldier told Contreras one day, "I can't keep quiet any longer. The Captain went into your house. He asked to speak to Isabel, alone, then tried to assault her. The lady resisted and the Captain struck her so hard that she had a miscarriage three hours afterwards."

When he heard this, Alonso went to the Captain's house and, drawing his sword, told him he was a vile excuse for a gentleman. The Captain drew his sword too, but Contreras gave him a thrust in the chest which felled him. Then he fled.

When in 1608 Contreras was accused of the arms incident of Hornacho, his flight was one of the things that made him most suspect. Alonso in his manliness did not wish to say why he had left, so it was suspected that the

Moors had paid him to leave and say nothing of their cache.

He crossed Italy, placing himself at the command of the Duke of Feria. For five years he fought the Turks as captain of the Duke's galleons. In the meantime he had married a rich and beautiful widow, a native of Madrid living in Sicily. Such was his loving respect for her that he never wore his hat in her presence even in the street.

One day in Palermo his little page asked him innocently: "Sir, in Spain do relatives kiss the wives of other relatives? Because Don Lope kissed milady and she showed him her garter."

The marriage did not last long. Contreras became a widower. He became a widower when he surprised his adored wife with Lope. He became a widower upon piercing them both with one sword thrust in their adulterous bed, with the skill of a naturalist impaling two butterflies for his collection.

Alonso fled Sicily and went back to Spain, hoping to become a captain there and perhaps find new experiences which would make him forget the old ones. If chance had made him escape from Spain after the arms incident, chance again brought him back five years later. It was then 1608. Shortly after his return the Moors started to revolt and the Decree of Expulsion was passed. The needle of fate, making Alonso come back to Spain just at this time, pointed now with a really dangerous insistence to the cache of Hornacho.

Seated on the ground in the ravine, Alonso was dismayed to think that all the roads he had followed in his youth led to the same point of departure: Hornacho.

Am I then fated to this? he wondered.

The sun shed its last rays, and Contreras went on reviewing the phantoms of the past, shuffling them over in his mind: ship-boardings, flights, seductions, intrigues, deaths, warm lips, warm bodies, naked loving arms, all different, all desirable. Suddenly in the midst of them peace had come to him. Alonso came to terms with himself and resolved to serve God in the desert, never thinking that his hermitage would be one more step toward the caves of Hornacho. No more warm bodies. No more deaths. No more courts or palaces. He bought the equipment of a hermit, hair shirt and scourge, sackcloth to make a robe, a sundial, penitential books and a skull. Then he started out for Moncayo. When asked where he was going he replied, "To serve another King, for I am tired."

Alonso remembered his seven months of the penitential life with emotion. His diet was bread, herbs and water. He was called Brother Alonso de la Madre de Dios. He was very happy, never sad or depressed.

If they hadn't taken me out of that the way they did, he brooded now, I would have stayed on there.

But they did take him away. He recalled his dismay at seeing an armed mob approaching his hermitage. They came as though they were preparing to attack a fortress. While he stood there with his rosary and staff they seized him and led him away. The local people who had come out to watch the crowd shouted, "This is the King of the Moors!"

They took him to prison where they questioned him about the discovery of arms five years before. They led him into a room hung with tapestries. Two candles stood on a table with a crucifix, an inkstand and paper. Nearby was a rack and beside it the torturer, the mayor and notary. The torturer ordered him to strip. Then, laying him on the rack they tied the cords and began to tighten them. They asked who he had delivered the arms to.

"I know that they gave you and your Captain four thousand ducats to keep quiet," said the mayor.

Alonso answered, "That's a lie! My Captain knew no more about it than the Sultan of Turkey."

"Another twist," ordered the mayor.

It seemed to Alonso that these memories were trying to swarm out like ugly insects from their hole. How the wheel of fortune turns, he thought. He got up and brushed the dust from his clothes. Who could have told me that after thirty years the people would once more call me King of the Moors!

The creaking of a branch startled him. It was a dog sniffing at rubbish. Night was falling. The distance had turned gray and the gold threads that the sun had been weaving sank in the water of the Tagus. The sun set behind the plain. He had to go back. It was time for the night watch to begin their rounds and it would not be wise for a fugitive like him to be seen. He slowly climbed the pine-topped ridge which leads from the river to the city. The first stars winked at him, but he did not see them. Alonso de Contreras walked blindly toward his destiny like a man foredoomed.

III

Alonso went to the old inn called La Posada de la Sangre. In the main plaza peddlers were gathering up their wares. Groups of men were chatting animatedly in the coolness of evening. But the plaza did not have the liveliness of thirty years ago when Alonso first knew it, for Toledo, like many other Spanish cities, had lost more than half its population after the expulsion of the Moors. The moon had not yet risen and the Alcazar of Toledo stood out majestically above the shadows.

Alonso, thinking that he was unknown, since he had neither debts nor enemies in Toledo, walked straight into the Posada. Inside were tables and chairs, wine spilled and unspilled, girls clutched and unclutched, and noise, lots of noise. Everyone in the patio turned to look at him. He was not exactly dressed for anonymity. His Italian boots, brightly colored Grecian breeches, elaborate green doublet laden with flamboyant decorations and crossed by the ribbon of the Order of Malta, topped by a vermilion cloak like the tail of a pheasant in mating time, was not quite the costume to choose for concealment among these simple people. The shabbiness of his hat with its faded yet aggressive feather did nothing to diminish his dashing figure. Contreras really did not give a damn how much they stared at him as long as no one recognized him. But someone did, almost immediately.

"Don Alonso! Don Alonso!"

Contreras did not turn around. Deliberately and feigning calm, he turned slowly and went out again.

Someone was behind him and the Captain, quickening his pace, ducked into a cobbled alley. But his pursuer came after him calling, "Don Alonso! Don Alonso!"

He turned a corner quickly and waited, pressed up against the wall, his hand ready on his sword. Suddenly the pursuer came around the corner, almost into him.

"Don Al—"

"Be quiet," said Alonso in his steely low voice, "or I'll make you quiet."

"Sir," came the whisper, "don't you recognize me?"

"No."

"I am Luigi."

"I don't know you."

"Luigi! I was your page in Palermo, sir. Remember — the one who told you about your wife's love affair with — "

"I don't remember. That was a hundred years ago."

"A hundred years — no, sir, just twenty-seven. I was eight years old at the time."

Alonso studied him briefly. Then turned to go, saying, "Well, good luck to you, boy, and go with God — I'm in a hurry."

"Don Al — "

"Shut up! Shut up or I'll cut out your tongue!"

"Sir, who are you running from?"

"From my shadows."

"Are your shadows the constables?"

"Listen, Luigi. You mustn't tell anyone you've seen me. You mustn't call me by my name. My life depends on it."

"Who have you killed, sir?"

"Not that this time, Luigi. I am just accused of being the King of the Moors, that's all."

The young man went pale. Night had closed in on Toledo. The only light glimmering in the shadows was a lamp before a mural of the Madonna.

"Of the Moors!" whispered Luigi, "God has set me in your path. I am the only one who can save you."

Alonso looked him up and down. Luigi was no longer the boy who had spied on his mistress twenty-seven years ago, but a full-grown man and willing, it would seem, to help him. Luigi smiled, standing his ground under the scrutiny. The footsteps of the night watch hammered on the cobbles of a nearby street.

"Follow me, sir."

Alonso hesitated a moment, then shrugged his shoulders and motioned Luigi on. They went down several streets so narrow that the feeble glow of the night scarcely seemed to reach them. Finally Luigi stopped at a door and knocked on it three times.

"Who's there?" asked a cautious voice.

"Friends," replied the Italian.

The bolts were drawn with squeaking protests and the door opened.

"God bless you, Luigi!" said a cloaked figure out of the shadows.

"May He be with you always and guide your steps," said Luigi.

Contreras followed the two men into the house. They went down a passageway and a flight of stairs into a large room. Luigi lit lamps, then turned to Contreras.

"How you've changed, sir!"

"Twenty-seven years have not passed in vain. You were a rather delicate little boy, Luigi. Now you have become strong."

"You are still strong, sir."

"That's the general tragedy, Luigi." Contreras smiled ruefully. "Some like you have *become* strong, others like me are *still* strong. Oh, Luigi, my lad, how many memories you awaken!"

"I hope, sir, that they are happy ones."

"Memories are always sad, Luigi. If they remind you of happy things they're sad because they are finished. One remembers only the things one has lost."

"You *are* melancholy, sir."

"I have my reasons." Contreras started to loosen his belt and take off his sword. Then he stopped. "Whose house is this?"

"Mine."

Contreras handed him his sword and sat down. "Do you live alone?"

"No."

"Whom do you live with?"

"With my father-in-law."

"And your wife?"

"She died."

"Ah!"

Luigi went out with Alonso's sword, cape and doublet. The Captain looked around him. The room was a cellar. Its rich Arabian carpet contrasted with the modest furniture. The house must have originally belonged to Moors.

High on the wall was a transom which probably gave light during the daytime, but now it was as black as the street they had left. Contreras heard voices and sprang up when he heard footsteps coming down the stairs toward this room.

The former page came in presently with a short man dressed in black, middle-aged, distinguished-looking, his deepset eyes small and penetrating. He had a hawk nose, skin as dry-looking as parchment, and a short white beard. Luigi introduced them: Don Fernando Valenzuela was Luigi's father-in-law.

"Luigi has told me," said Don Fernando in a voice as clipped as his beard, "that they have made grave accusations against you, although you are a man of honor. In Palermo — "

Luigi blushed to his ears as Contreras looked at him severely and said, "Affairs of honor are so delicate that one should be silent about them."

"Sir," Luigi answered, "only my devotion to you led me to bring you here when I knew of the danger you were in. As the accusation has to do with Moors, only Don Fernando and I can help you. But in order to do so we must know more."

"Luigi has spoken well," said Don Fernando.

"Luigi has not spoken well. The story of the Moors is one thing, but old tales that Luigi knows have nothing to do with my present predicament."

Valenzuela scratched his head and went on with the doggedness of old age: "Whether the two stories are related or not remains to be seen. As for me, I would be

interested to know how you two came to know each other
and up to what point Luigi should feel obliged to endan-
ger his life and mine by saving yours, Captain.'

"Sir — " pleaded Luigi.

Contreras stared thoughtfully at them, hesitated an instant, then said, "Very well."

Luigi and Valenzuela listened to his story without miss-
ing a syllable. Luigi nodded from time to time, his face
reflecting his emotions as each incident of the affair was
related. Valenzuela on the other hand did not move a
muscle, but his eyes closed now and then as though to
picture the scenes.

"Now, my good friends," concluded Contreras, "the
important thing is for you to go to my main witness,
Vilches, and ask him to come to me. He will stand by me
in this crisis."

"Sir," said Luigi, "Vilches is a good friend of mine!
His tavern is just nearby at the foot of the Alcázar. If you
like I can go to him right now and tell him. He's a good
man and we can trust him."

"Remember, Luigi, the walls have ears."

Luigi smiled and left.

After what seemed like hours, there was a knock at
the door.

"Who goes there?" called Don Fernando as he went
upstairs.

"Friends!" came Luigi's voice from outside.

"May the grace of God fall on you, Luigi!" said the old
man as he ran the bolts.

"May He be with you always and guide your steps,"

panted Luigi. He stumbled down the stairs and the Captain caught him to keep him from falling.

Contreras said laughingly, "By the life of Satan, your greeting is elegant! Is this the Toledo custom?"

Luigi was pale and trembling.

"This is no time for jests! Sir, you are in the greatest danger. Osorio is in Toledo — Vilches has been murdered, and you are publicly accused of killing him in order to do away with a witness to your treason!"

"You lie!" roared Contreras. "Vilches was a witness *against* Osorio — the Commissar is the only one who profits by his death!"

"The city is in an uproar, and everybody is searching the churches because you are supposed to be hiding in one of them."

Contreras dashed upstairs and came back buckling on his sword and doublet.

"For the love of God, sir, have you lost your mind?" shouted Luigi. "Where are you going? All the roads are blocked."

Contreras started toward the door but Luigi stepped in front of him. "They say they are hunting you in groups of six because you were known in Naples as the best swordsman in the kingdom."

Contreras smiled confidently. "Then six are too few."

Suddenly Valenzuela put a finger to his lips. They all looked up at the transom. They could hear many voices and people running in the street. Then the roll of drums silenced the voices.

"*In the name of the King let it be proclaimed to the*

citizens of the noble and imperial city of Toledo that a great malefactor has taken refuge here. He passes as a Captain, calls himself a Knight of Malta and answers to the name of Alonso de Roa y Contreras. Let this be a summons to all who have seen him or know who has seen him in Toledo, or in the nearby mountains or woods . . ."

Luigi and Valenzuela did not take their eyes off the Captain. He was standing with head erect, his feet apart as though to keep his balance and his chin moving as though he were chewing.

"This is the reward for my services!" And he put a strand of beard between his teeth.

The crier continued:

"The worst malefactor who has trod Christian earth. Excommunicated by the Church, one hundred times a murderer, robber of women, a leader of Moors, traitor to the King . . ."

Contreras was very pale, and so quiet that it was frightening. The crier went on.

"Put out the lamp," said Contreras suddenly.

When Luigi and Valenzuela did not move, Contreras quickly blew out the lamp and the room was dim in the yellowish light that came through the transom from the street.

"What are you going to do, sir?"

"I'll wash my honor clean or sup with Christ!" Unsheathing his sword he dashed up the stairs.

"We are dead!" Luigi called after him. "Oh you madman, is this the way you repay us?"

In the street, by the light of a torch, the crier could still be heard reading the proclamation in a singsong voice. Fourteen or fifteen boys were around him, six armed constables, and three torchbearers and a drummer.

Contreras' voice was used to being heard above the noisiest storms and sea battles. Now he shouted from the shadows, freezing the crier's singsong in his throat: "The son of a whore lies who says these things, and the traitor lies who ordered him to say them!"

Luigi put his hand to his mouth and his teeth bit into his knuckles. Valenzuela sank into a chair and closed his eyes. In the silence that followed they heard slow advancing footsteps on the cobbles.

"In the King's name!" shouted a voice. Then the noise of running and shouts and the clash of six swords on one.

"Válame la Virgen! " suddenly cried a voice, gurgling with blood. "Confession!"

Then another screamed: "Jesús!"

There was the crash of breaking glass, then darkness. "Torches! Torches! More light!"

Again running, more groans, and at last silence . . . The street was dark. Two minutes passed which seemed like centuries to Luigi. Then the front door creaked open and from the top of the stairs came Contreras' triumphant low voice: "Christ preferred to cleanse my honor than to sup with me!"

Valenzuela whispered, "Close the shutters and light the lamp."

Luigi obeyed.

In one hand the smiling Contreras held his sword wet to the hilt and in the other, torn and bloodstained, the proclamation.

IV

Valenzuela left the room and came back presently with a *bota* of wine. "Drink," he said to Contreras, "it will do you good."

The Captain raised his elbow and drank. Almost immediately his eyes began to cloud. He looked glassily at his friends for a moment and fell to the floor. Luigi gave a great sigh.

"We have to work quickly — there's no time to lose."

They carried Contreras' body between them to the kitchen. Luigi removed the ashes and logs from the hearth and lifted the trap door hidden beneath them.

When Contreras woke up he wanted to move but he could not. He wanted to speak but he could not. He opened his eyes. Little white lights were going on and off. When he closed his eyes the lights went on in his head, multiplying like fireworks. His blood was pounding in his veins and his brain seemed ready to explode to the rhythm of a savage tomtom. Little by little the lights faded away, the noises quieted down. These were replaced by lighted torches and the murmur of prayers. He sat up. Everything was going around.

I am drunk, he thought. A few feet away some men were kneeling on the floor. The figures kept superimposing themselves on each other so that at first there were five, then four, then two. All of a sudden he vomited, convulsively as though he were losing all his insides. He felt better.

"I hate to see him like this," he heard a voice whisper.

"If we set him free," murmured another voice, "he will end on the gallows."

"And ourselves with him."

"Where — " Contreras began.

Luigi came up to him. "You are with me, sir. Don't be afraid."

They were in a richly carpeted cavern. At one end were various sacks and weights and two coffins.

"Am I going to die?"

"No."

At the other end a stairway led to a trap door opening in the cave's roof. Don Fernando Valenzuela, his hands stained with pitch, came and went fussing with medical concoctions. Contreras, sitting on the floor, his hands tied behind him and his legs bound at the ankles, watched him.

"Are you Moors; is that it?"

Don Fernando turned, looked steadily into his eyes and, without paying any attention to the question, said, "Captain, if we have resorted to guile to put you in this position it is only for your good. You are a reckless man and unfortunately your sword is as good as your judgment is bad. Consider, for your welfare and ours, whether it wasn't insane to disembowel several constables, rob a crier, terrify a whole city, compromise your friends and in every way strengthen the Secretary's opinion that he is right to hunt down a man like you. At this late hour the city is still in a turmoil. The news will soon reach Madrid confirming the suspicion that you are in Toledo, and mind you, it was only a suspicion. Nobody was sure till today. You can count the hours before they take you. And once they take you you won't have time to say so much as a Paternoster before you die as a traitor to the King and as a King of the Moors."

"And so you are going to turn me over — "

"No."

"Then may they hang me if I understand you!"

Valenzuela turned back to his potions. Luigi squatted in front of Contreras. He told him of his father-in-law's amazing learning and the rare talents with which heaven had endowed him.* Valenzuela could read the stars, he knew the language of animals. He knew how to bring seeming corpses back to life . . . (Luigi lowered his voice) he also knew . . . (Contreras leaned forward to hear better) how to keep the souls of the newly dead in their bodies for as long as thirty days.

"You're lying, heretic!" exclaimed Contreras.

But Luigi went on: "On one occasion some persecuted Moors begged Don Fernando to give them death that they might escape so he did it."

* If this were a fictional tale it would be important to know the background of this intriguing character Valenzuela and how he came by his extraordinary learning. Unfortunately, we know only what Contreras himself heard and observed about him in this short time he knew him. So many questions come to mind. Was he renowned or did he practice and study in secret? Did he leave any written papers on his experiments? What exactly were those "potions" and how had he come by the knowledge to mix them?

Valenzuela broke in with a smile.

"Luigi doesn't put it very scientifically, I'm afraid. The whole city was looking for them — like you — because a high price had been put on their heads, although not as high as yours, for they were only Moors, not King of the Moors like you."

Contreras tried to break his bonds. But Valenzuela, ignoring Contreras' struggles, continued. He described point by point how he killed his protégés — an apparent death, although it had all the effects and characteristics which accompany real death. The lungs ceased to function, the heart to beat. The blood no longer ran in the veins. The Moors were then delivered to justice by Valenzuela who claimed to have poisoned them. He would refuse the award in exchange for permission to bury them in an estate he had near the city. He would, of course, confess to having killed them, alleging that it was for the good of the country. But he would add that he could not forget that they were human beings, and that he wanted to pacify his conscience by keeping their bodies and praying for their souls. Valenzuela kept his promise faithfully and buried them deep in a crypt on his estate in the presence of the mayor and the notary. They remained buried for thirty-two days, at the end of which Don Fernando, aided by his daughter, disinterred them and gave them back their lives. The Moors recovered in a few days from their false death and then, dressed as priests, they sailed for South America where they had become prosperous and respected.

"And so," Valenzuela said suddenly, "Contreras, here is your choice: to die on the gallows as a traitor or to have

Luigi hand you over to the law — dead. Just to see you dead will be enough for Osorio. Afterwards you can be free to find your other witnesses and draw up your accusation so that at last you will see Osorio's head roll off the scaffold."

He returned to his tasks, adding casually: "You may meditate for a short while, Captain, on whether you want this done willingly or by force."

The silence following these words was prolonged and tense. Luigi held his breath. Contreras' lungs heaved. Finally he said, "Willingly, by God!"

Luigi gave a sigh of relief. "Thank God."

The casket in which they placed Alonso's body was made of iron and weighed more than a cannon. Three days' diet of nothing but potions and purgatives and emetics had brought him to such a state that he might have died anyway without artificial intervention. They bled him till he was so weak that he could only sigh an oath while Valenzuela and Luigi, with the learning of doctors and the patience of hermits, went on with their preliminary procedure.

They covered every part of his body with a thick greasy paste. Then they wrapped him in a special cloth which they painted with a kind of tar. Only his face was left uncovered, and this emerged from the shroud like an agonized soul peering out of its own special hell.

"Do you wish anything, Captain?"

"My sword," murmured Contreras. "Bury it with me."

Luigi nodded.

"May the Madonna of Mercy bring me to a blessed port. Amen!"

Then Valenzuela carefully felt the Captain's back with his fingers. He made three marks on it: between his shoulder-blades, the back of his neck and his coccyx. Then he took a small hammer and gave a sharp blow on each of these spots. The body, as though moved by a spring, became as rigid as a drawn bow. They turned him over. The face contracted, his lips became pale, his eyes sank in, his nostrils contracted . . .

Alonso opened his eyes and his brain became less foggy. He saw a strange face leaning over him. No, it could not be Luigi staring at him like that, even though Valenzuela's sorcery probably could change features if he felt like it. This face was clean-shaven; the eyes were small and covered by glass pieces attached to the nose, porous and shiny.

Contreras heard his own voice speaking from miles away: "Go—hurry now, wizard, and give me my life."

The man's face contracted with a twisted grin and he went away. At a few paces off Alonso could see him better. He was dressed in clothes which Alonso had never come across in all his travels. His legs were encased in a pair of flannel tubes resembling the barrels of cannons. His torso was covered by a waistcoat that reached to the hips, and his arms were tubular also. Alonso thought he might be a monk, for the cloth of his costume was dark. But the shaven face and the knotted sort of belt at his throat puzzled him.

"Who — are — you?" he asked.

"The doctor," answered Salvador Yuste.

"Am I going to die?"

"No."

"How long have I slept?"

"A long time."

"Luigi — was right . . ."

Silence. Alonso and Salvador stared at each other.

"Are you thirsty?"

"Yes — Where is Luigi?"

"I'm afraid I don't know."

"The Inquisition . . ."

"Here, drink."

"But — how long have I slept?"

"As I said, a long time."

"How long? Answer, dog!"

"It's October."

"Christ! Luigi was right!"

Contreras closed his eyes as though he were going to sleep again.

Salvador went quickly out of the room. He crossed the shadowy corridor and hurried downstairs to a telephone booth. The night watchman asked: "Any news, Don Salvador?"

"I have to make a phone call."

"And that madman, how is he doing?"

"He is waking up."

The doctor closed the door of the booth after him.

"Waking up," the porter murmured shaking his head, "Lord bless us!"

(End of Editor's Preface. What follows is Antonio Cornejo's account of the Contreras affair.)

CHAPTER ONE

I T WAS Saturday night. The Chief had sent down several examples of his idea of a "splendid piece" and I was trying valiantly to inject some semblance of life and imagination into them.

The Chief and I hadn't been doing too well lately — ever since the appearance of the mysterious man in the seventeenth century casket and my first article about same. It seems I had violated his favorite creed, one he was wont to jam down the throat of every new man on the paper.

"See here, young man," he'd bluster, "you may exaggerate on the front page, but not lie. In the inside pages, you may lie but not exaggerate."

The Chief would accept any news, even though false, if it *seemed* true to life; on the other hand he would not publish anything that did not seem true to life even though it happened to be Gospel. Naturally, this brought him great success during the World War. He directed his own war from his desk; it had nothing whatsoever to do with the actual war being fought but it was what his readers wanted.

The night the first report of the sensational "resurrection" was phoned in I happened to be on duty, in complete charge as night editor. I took advantage of the fact by slapping the story onto the front page without even checking it. I protected myself with many "it is saids" and a couple of "some people claims" but still the Chief wanted to fire me the next day. The Board, however, overrode him, because our little paper which had rarely been seen out of barbershops was suddenly gobbled up on every street corner; it was being avidly read everywhere, from the anterooms of Ministries to convent cloisters.

Bolstered by the success of my subsequent articles, the clamor of the publicity, and supported by the labor laws which make it hard to fire a man, I was all set to defy the Chief and champion the great and noble cause of the "resurrected man" of the Almudena Cemetery even if I had to start my own paper to do it. This was my crusading state of mind when the telephone rang that evening.

"Is this Cornejo, author of the Contreras articles?"

"Speaking."

There was a pause.

"Who's this?" I finally had to ask.

"Dr. Yuste."

About now is as good a place as any to identify myself.

I am a journalist, bachelor, ambitious, and not a complete fool, if I say so myself. I began my journalistic career in 1934 reporting traffic accidents, that probably being the reason I was made editor of an automobile magazine published by the State. It folded shortly thereafter, and my good luck began. I held down one newspaper job after another until I landed the present one where I suddenly seemed to become inspired and became an indispensable factotum overnight.

My technique, while perhaps not earth-shaking in other countries, was new in Spain. Not for me were the stereotyped shots of the outsides of burning buildings. When our photographer refused to come with me, I took the pictures myself: in the flames.

My first big success came after the mine caved in near Getafe burying five workers. When, after three days of excavating, the rescue brigade was able to reach the men, they found them talking calmly with me. I'd had to squeeze my way through a flooded passage, but the exclusive I came out with was worth a little danger and wetting.

After a few months my reputation on the newspaper was established. The condescending smile which had accompanied the phrase "Cornejo stuff" changed quickly to "Only Cornejo can handle this job."

It was chance that caused me to be the first to get my hands on the Contreras story, and I am the only one able to inform the public about the complete truth of it all. The absurdity of some of the things that have been said is what's impelled me to give the real story at last.

"Listen carefully, and don't interrupt," Dr. Yuste told me that night on the telephone. "What I have to say might be of the greatest personal interest to you. What time do you get off?"

"If it's that important, right now."

"Right now, then. And not a word to anyone."

"Hell, Doctor, you can trust me, I'm a reporter."

"That's just it," said the doctor, and he hung up.

When I arrived at the hospital, Dr. Yuste was waiting for me at the door.

"Come up," he said tensely.

My professional heart was pounding; I had the feeling that I was on the brink of what I could build up into my biggest story yet. I went up the stairs quickly after Dr. Yuste.

We went down the corridor and into the room of Alonso de Contreras.

He lay on the bed, naked as the day he was born, his skin so pale he looked very dead. He appeared to be unusually tall, the width of his rib case and the great expansion of shoulders indicating an athlete. He had a huge gray beard which had been snipped here and there by the police for analysis and he was so thin that all his bones showed prominently under his skin.

The phrase of a lead for my story began to take shape in my mind —

In the excitement I hadn't brought a pencil and I was on the point of asking the doctor for his pen when his next words stopped me.

"He and I," he said pointing at the patient with a thin forefinger, "we need your help."

Then he offered me a chair, sitting down himself, and watching my eyes to see the effect of his words upon me.

I sat down and squirmed a bit as I felt his gaze upon me.

Yuste was a strange man. He was under medium height, but his head was way out of proportion; he had either too much head or too little body. He had a thick nose perpetually pearled with sweat. His brilliant eyes looked at me over a pair of spectacles clipped to his nose. His mouth, which was almost lipless, seemed to have been made by a sudden slash with a surgeon's scalpel. His bristly hair was cut short. He seemed at first a crude peasant type but his hands were delicate and as well cared for as a woman's.

"Doctor," I began casually, "I'm sure you must realize that I really don't believe in this — this resurrection, shall we call it?"

"But you're the one who's been defending it the loudest!"

I shrugged and gave him a knowing look. "Business is business, Doctor."

He fixed me with those agate eyes of his and said slowly and mysteriously, "Think what the future business could be, my friend."

He then put a proposition to me which would have convinced any ordinary person that here was a mentally disturbed man. I thought it was wonderful.

He suggested that we abduct the body of this "reliving caballero," as he persisted in calling our supine friend, hide it, and thus prevent any police investigation and meddling pseudo-scientific interference which might lead to Dr. Lafuente's gloomy and unimaginative prediction: "Jail or the insane asylum."

The doctor would use the time that we had him hidden

to prove to the scientific world the possibility, not of a resurrection, of course, but of a successful artificially induced deathlike state; for although no one knew why or for how long, Dr. Yuste was convinced that his subject had been in a medically induced and genuine state of suspension for a long, long time.

My job would be to control public opinion by defending the doctor's ideas and to explain his experiments in the press. It looked as though he were rallying himself to drag in all sorts of arguments to convince me, and he was surprised when I replied: "Don't strain yourself, Doctor. You don't have to go into any routine about how I'd be helping science and humanity and all that. It's quite enough to appeal to me in the name of — of literature, let's say. And believe me, you don't have to try to convince me that this fellow's a survivor of the Dark Ages — I'm being convinced more and more by the second."

He frowned when I winked. He seemed extremely keyed up and ran on about how the man had spoken and what he'd said and so forth, but I really wasn't listening too well. I was busy thinking about the day when I would spill this story, the story that was already taking shape as I looked triumphantly at the huge sleeping form which no other newspaperman in the world had laid eyes on. There he was — I could reach out and touch him!

I could not know then that all my future would from then on be tied up with his destiny, for better or worse, until death.

CHAPTER TWO

As THE FIRST contours of the Pyrenees turned the road into a writhing snake, Dr. Yuste's eyes began to sparkle. The car climbed jerkily, panting like an exhausted horse, the tires screamed on the curves, and we had to stop several times to put water from the streams into the boiling radiator.

Yuste was not listening to my lyrical commentary on the scenery. I could see that his brain was working at a furious rate, as though it was already working on his laboratory experiments.

I had plunged into this adventure like Napoleon into war: "First I commit myself, then I think about it." Yuste, on the other hand, was most precise in his reactions; he had solutions for every small problem that crossed our path as though he had foreseen them all during long hours of meditation.

We had stolen one of the hospital ambulances (whose

only function was to take Dr. Lafuente to his country house on weekends). From time to time I turned to look through the glass partition at Alonso asleep, his body strapped to the stretcher. Dense clouds began to cover the sky, and the temperature dropped as we went on, threatening a storm.

"If it snows," Yuste said suddenly, "everything will be just fine."

We crossed a rocky gully, so narrow that the road ran dangerously near the river gorge. Yuste took the curve with less caution than he should have, but we made it somehow. We passed Sort with its ruined castle. The valley opened gradually; dominating it, crowned by threatening dark clouds, rose the solitary crests of Montseny de Pillars.

"What time is it?" asked Yuste.

"Twelve o'clock. We've been on the road for nine hours."

The mountain landscape changed as we went along, as though on turning each curve we were turning the page of a book of colored prints. We left the valley of Noguera behind, and now the air, the deep green of the pastures, the peacefulness of the cattle, even the smoky breath of the horses that watched us, gave a sense of altitude. The black poplars, almonds and small pines gave way to pastures quietly climbing the mountain. It was a landscape that was placid, damp, tender, almost feminine, crossed by slow streams. Higher up the scenery hardened. Lonely fir trees on the outskirts of meadows were advance sentinels for the forest.

The car climbed, wrenched around the curves by the doctor. It would draw deep breaths on the levels and descents till the road, suddenly rearing like a horse, cut its speed, and the motor coughed like a sick man.

"Come on, come on!" was Yuste's idea of encouraging it.

"It's raining," I said.

"It's snowing," Yuste corrected. He stopped the car and we got out. The air cut into my skin like icy pins. Coming from the north, not falling gently but whipped in sideways by the wind, the fine snow filled the creases of the mountains, the crevices of stones, the ruts in the road.

"We must hurry," said the doctor. "In two hours the Pass of Bonaigua will be closed."

We went on. After the Pass at the very top, the road plunged down dangerously. A veil completely hid the Valley of Arán, and my eyes, without the scenery to rest them, filled with sleep. I made the rest of the trip sound asleep, although not as sound as our passenger in the rear.

Yuste woke me up. We had arrived. We were in the clearing of a forest. I had never seen country like this and at first I thought it was a continuation of my dream. Giant spruce trees rose from every side, and the snow fell in large flakes among their branches. An old man wearing a beret down to his eyebrows was greeting us with evident pleasure.

"My boy . . . so long since I last saw you! I knew you'd come back!"

His daughter, tall and silent, brought us warm water

for washing. The old man told us that it was a wonder we had been able to get through the Pass of Bonaigua. In a few hours it would have vanished from sight. The Valley of Arán would be shut off behind that mountain wall; and in it were Alonso de Contreras and ourselves, isolated from the rest of Spain, from the rest of the world, till the spring sun would decide to unwrap the white shroud from the Pass six months later.

Salvador Yuste had even foreseen the snow!

CHAPTER THREE

THE RETREAT in the Valley of Arán chosen by Dr. Yuste to hide Alonso de Contreras was in the heart of a forest near the French border and not far from Andorra. In this refuge, far from the reach of police investigation, Yuste was free to save his patient and to study him.

I, in the meantime, was to plan the press campaign which was to precede Yuste's arrival in Madrid. It was good for Contreras himself too, said Yuste, because he would not suffer the same shock of change from his century to ours that he would have done waking up in the hectic fever of a great modern city. Dr. Yuste could not have chosen a better hiding place.

During his long walks the doctor used to wander toward the Barranco del Lobo. Here the forest suddenly broke up and threw itself down a rocky cliff. From there one could see the valley, crossed by the Garonne swollen by many streams. Beyond the valley, peaks and clouds, snows and rivers, rise the Mountains of the Damned with their two heads, Maladetta and Aneto. Legend says that in ancient times some shepherds living in these mountains denied help to a beggar who appeared there asking for alms. They say that the beggar was the Son of God and as a punishment he changed the two shepherds into boulders.

Dr. Yuste used to try to reconstruct the figures of the shepherds in the profiles of these peaks. He felt the need to distract himself with the landscape, but it was no use. All his ideas, try as he would to let them wander, were fatally attracted to the one magnet that drew all our thoughts toward it: Alonso de Contreras.

Since leaving the hospital Contreras had remained in a stupor, briefly interrupted by moments of lucidity in which he would ask, as though obsessed, the reason for his sleep.

"How long have I slept?" he asked again one day.

"When did you begin to sleep?" the doctor countered.

"Luigi . . . Luigi put me to sleep on . . . on the Feast of the Visitation." And he added feebly, "Where am I? Are you . . . are you Spanish? Where am I? How long have I slept?"

"I am Spanish," the doctor answered gently, "and I am your friend. My name is Salvador Yuste."

"Yuste!" murmured the patient nostalgically. "That is where the Emperor died!"

There was a long silence.

"I am thirsty . . . I am thirsty . . ."

And he fell asleep again.

Day after day the doctor watched the man's every reaction, fearing for his patient's life, dreading a final sleep as much as a decisive waking. Now that the climax seemed to be approaching, Yuste both desired and feared the end of that unnatural death pang and the change from apparent death to real life.

The first nourishment was very light and given at long intervals. The first steps were for only thirty seconds daily for the first weeks; the patient would lean on the doctor or me, for his legs would not obey him. Yuste had coached the gamewarden and his daughter, giving them the facts by doses, as though they were pills of thought, so that they would not upset the small mental world of the patient with the tremendous truth. Everything, steps, nourishment, ideas, was measured, weighed and thoroughly thought out by the doctor. When Contreras slept Yuste spoke in his ear as though to direct his dreams, preparing Contreras' subconscious for the truth.

During his long walks the doctor would review the progress of his patient and make his future plans. But Contreras had his plans too. When he was convinced that none of us were members of the Inquisition, nor had anything to do with Osorio, nor even with Valenzuela and Luigi, he concluded that his Toledan friends had managed to transport his body to this place, but then their crime had been discovered and they had been forced to flee, abandoning him.

So he decided to stay quietly where he was till he should have recovered his strength, and then confide in his physician, telling him how he must reach Lisbon and set sail from there on an affair of honor. He finally did confide in him but, on detecting a certain reluctance in his new friend, he saw that it was best to tell him the entire story from beginning to end, including the trick used to deceive his persecutors, and his plans for the future.

And that was how we first came to know the history of the man and how he came to be in the coffin, which has already been related.

Contreras' reactions to the reality surrounding him while he was still uncontaminated by the germs of our century are of inestimable value, not only for the insight they gave into his character but for a comparative study of the two mental centuries which began to clash in him from that time on.

Dr. Yuste finally felt obliged to use the one argument that would quench his growing desire to escape: he told him the truth. He told him that Valenzuela and Luigi no longer existed, nor did the Inquisition, and that Osorio had gone to his Last Judgment three centuries ago, so that there was no reason to escape or to avenge himself on anybody.

Contreras was not amazed or shocked or frightened as we expected. His face lit with joy. He gazed at the roof and the walls with the nervous and childish expression of a blind man recovering his sight.

"This is no trick, is it?" he said, and he asked the doctor to repeat the good news. Which he did, twice.

"This means," the doctor started to say, "that . . ."

"This means," interrupted Contreras, "that I shall soon be an Admiral!"

Had the Captain really understood what the doctor had told him? Was he able to appreciate the extent of its meaning? Was he so unaware that he could not comprehend the tragedy of having one's coffin separated from one's cradle by an abyss in which he had not lived? The frightening thing about many of this man's reactions was his lack of surprise at happenings which shake us today, and yet at the same time the superstitious terror with which he regarded trivialities of our everyday living.

When several months later we told him about the hydrogen bomb, radar, the splitting of the atom, NATO, and the recently created agency for interplanetary trips, he was not in the least upset. But he trembled at running water, democracy, a doorbell or a girl on a bicycle.

And when did I, the arch cynic, begin believing in the truth of the Contreras tale?

The account Dr. Yuste told me of his first talk with his patient that night he called me out of my office decided me to become his accomplice in the abduction of the body. I was dazzled by the thought of exploiting such an unusual case; but I did not stop to think seriously about the possibility of its being really true.

After all, it was impossible! But in the Valley of Arán, during the months we lived there together, I gradually became convinced that all this was not a fable or a dream, nor a hoax. But when that creature, that phantom, turned into a real person with a name and a past, with even his *Memoirs* published years before his apparition, I felt, by a paradoxical reaction, the desperate desire not to believe *anything*, to flee from the evidence itself. Until then my belief in the man's resurrection was purely literary in character; I believed because it was an exciting thought that what I really didn't believe *might* be the truth. But when the overwhelming evidence began to penetrate I defended myself like a lion. I'd wake up in the morning convinced that it was all a tremendous fraud, but at night, after direct contact with Contreras, I'd go to bed with the opposite conviction.

As for the doctor, translating his scientific bewilderment into literary language, I compared his reaction to that of a poet singing odes to the water sprites on the banks of a stream; suddenly they materialize and express their willingness to live with him. When they were only a dream the poet believed in them. But now, when they're within reach, he dare not approach them, fearing to cross the border of the unreal world of fancy into the terrifying certainty of a real world of mental unbalance.

It was moving to see the contrast between Contreras' faith in his longevity after three centuries and the doubt of the man without whose help he wouldn't have been able to wake up in the twentieth century! The conflict between the doubt of the discoverer and the faith of the discovered represented the first clash between these two centuries: the skeptical twentieth and the miraculous seventeenth.

One day when the doctor and I were sitting with Contreras at the door of the cabin, the Captain asked the doctor what he was thinking.

"I'm not thinking," said Yuste, "I'm doubting."

"Doctor — friend, you have not lived long enough to

doubt," said Contreras in his quaint, archaic style of speaking. "May I ask what it is that you doubt?"

"A miracle."

"If you doubt a miracle then it does not exist, for miracles carry their own evidence with them."

"Then you believe in miracles?" the doctor asked, smiling.

"How could I not? I have lived through more than six of them!"

María, the gamewarden's daughter, sitting near them, stopped her mending.

"One of them," said Contreras, "took place during a battle with a Turkish ship in the waters of Alexandria. It lasted three hours, at the end of which we captured and sacked the ship and made slaves out of the survivors. The two hundred and fifty dead we threw into the sea. You know that if dead bodies in the sea be those of Moors or Turks they float with their faces down, facing the infernal regions, but Christians float face up. Well, I saw something that day that will make you see what it is to be a Christian. One of the Turkish dead was floating face up, which was very contrary to his race and religion. We were all speculating on this odd occurrence so we asked some of our Turkish captives the reason for it. They said that they had always suspected that man of being a Christian, for although he claimed to be a renegade, he was a baptized Frenchman and practiced his religion in secret. Tell me if it is not a miracle that God, before sending the dead to hell, should turn them around to see their faces first . . .

"Another miracle took place in Lampedusa, an island between Malta and Barbary. They say it is enchanted and that it is where King Rugero y Bradamonte fought a battle. That is only a fable to me. But what is not a fable is that there is a cave on the island where Christians venerate the image of a Madonna while the Turks venerate a Mohammedan hermit who is buried there. Both Christians and Turks take refuge in the cave when they are shipwrecked, in hope that a ship of their religion will save them. They all eat the food left them by Christian boats. But no boat, Turkish or Christian, dares take payment from those in the cave or seek the treasure it contains. If they were to do so their boats would not be able to leave port, even with a wind. Or they would sink. I tried and my boat sank . . ."

Dr. Yuste listened carefully to Contreras. The miracle that disturbed him was a different one. He felt transported by that man's evocation of a past in which miracles, as Contreras said, carried their own evidence with them. The man spoke so casually, so easily, so knowledgeably about events of ancient history!

"But these miracles are nothing compared to the great one I am going to tell you about. I was in Cambray with my regiment, a lieutenant at the time. One night it happened that I had sentry duty on the ramparts with a Mallorcan called Juan Jul. A courier came up to us and said that the King of France had been killed that day with two knife thrusts. It was decided that I should take the news to the governor. He had gone to bed. On hearing the news he was much alarmed because he knew the situation and the danger in which this would put the Spanish garrison. Next day the news was contradicted and everyone made fun of my companion and me, saying we must have dreamed it. Nine days afterwards Henry IV, King of France, was assassinated, exactly as the courier had told us. The assassin was a schoolmaster named François Ravaillac, native of Angoulême in Brittany. This happened on the 14th of May, 1610. The Spanish Ambassador in Paris was Don Iñigo de Cárdenas. It was thought that an angel had given me the news of the event before it happened so that the Spanish garrison might be prepared."

When Contreras had finished his story an icy breeze began to stir the boughs of the fir trees. It seemed as though some spirit had paralyzed our tongues, for neither the doctor nor I could say a word. María, who had been trembling all through Contreras' tale, lowered her eyes and went on with her mending. But the breeze changed to a wild wind sprinkled with snowflakes.

All night the invisible fingers of the wind clutched at the house as though trying to carry it off, to recover something there that belonged to it, something which the wind had forgotten centuries ago.

CHAPTER FOUR

HALF a year later: Madrid!

Completely oblivious to my gaze Alonso de Contreras, a vastly different Contreras, was dressing in front of the mirror. A large window overlooking the park let in streams of light, the laughter of children and the noise of traffic. In the closet were the half-dozen suits we had bought him along with the custom-made shirts, and the long row of expensive shoes. In the bathroom were all the concoctions necessary to a handsome man of the modern world. Contreras had learned how to manage soap, brush and comb, awkwardly at first, but now with ease. Realizing that he had forgotten something he was mentally reciting his lesson: First, the bath, then the teeth, then the shave, then the hair, then the hands and nails . . . He finally remembered what it was. He took the shaving lotion and patted it onto his face. There came a snort of pain.

"It stings! It stings!"

"Easy, Captain, easy! The day you learn not to bellow under a cold shower and when you use shaving lotion you'll begin to be a civilized man."

"The devil with it!" he said, with his good laugh. He took the scissors and began to trim his mustache as carefully as a good gardener trims the best box hedge in the garden.

Seeing Contreras like this, very much the gentleman, living like a Minister of State, I was thinking of the obstacles we had overcome so that he might live and dress like this. I too, incidentally, was dressing better.

Business isn't bad, Cornejo, not bad at all, I said to myself, not unjustifiably pleased. How much time had gone by since the snows had melted and Dr. Yuste had decided to come back to the Madrid Police before they should begin to look for him? Scarcely six months. Yet, as Contreras used to say: "How many times had the wheel of fortune turned for us!"

I had to laugh remembering the year we had spent since Contreras' appearance, six months in the Valley of Arán and six in Madrid.

"Splendid, Cornejo, splendid!" the Chief had said when I walked into his office after the Arán sojourn. He had completely forgotten that he didn't like me. He handed me a copy of the first installment of the series which the gamewarden had mailed for me in Andorra. "Six editions exhausted in six hours! The newsstands telephoned every half hour to say that people were grabbing the papers as soon as they came out. Send more, send more! My boy, we ran out, just plain ran out of paper!"

Really, the headlines the Chief honored me with were tremendous, no other word for it. POLICE RIGHT. YUSTE SNATCHED ALMUDENA MYSTERY BODY. This was subtitled with an impressive summary. *Sensational Report from our Special Correspondent: The motive for the kidnaping, according to the eminent scientist, was to allow him to study the case far from the interference of the hospital director. "After the hospital, either the jail or the insane asylum," says Dr. Lafuente, with monotonous regularity . . .*

The Chief told me about the success of my articles but he did not have to tell me about the success of our arrival in Madrid. Picture the scene:

Mediodía Station. Contreras stepped off the train handcuffed. It was I who, with the doctor's consent, had advised the police to do this. I told them they should take every precaution against a man as dangerous as the Captain. I was aware that in England a handcuffed man is looked on with suspicion, but in Spain the crowd always reacts in his favor. And what a reaction!

After discussing the plan with the doctor, we decided to have me leave the train first to work up the crowd. Also, I definitely did not want Contreras to be dressed in a good suit or to wear a tie. He had to be dressed so that his clothes looked borrowed, he had to look rather strange to the crowd. On the other hand, it would have been a trifle absurd for him to wear a costume of his own century.

Now, seeing him come off the train wearing corduroy

trousers and a workman's blouse, his beard jutting out beneath the big slouch hat of a country doctor, I inwardly applauded my own and Yuste's dramatic gifts. The crowd of curiosity-seekers gazed in wonder as Contreras stepped forward cautiously between two policemen. Directly behind him came Dr. Yuste dressed in black in a noble attitude of offended dignity.

"Really," I said in a startled voice to those near me, "the man with the beard looks like someone from another century." Then I ducked into another group to repeat the same thing.

"And the doctor," I added, "he looks brilliant!"

At the exit of the station some photographers stopped the group. The police posed. Ten or twelve photographers, some on their knees, some standing, began to shoot their pictures.

As the first flash bulb went off, Contreras, seeing what looked like firearms aimed at him, became alarmed. He broke loose from his guards, with one wrench of his powerful body, thrashed into the people in front of him, and landed in a pile of sacks and boxes. He glared out from this barricade with his manacled hands raised and ready to strike the first one to come near him.

The crowd, seized with panic, rolled back like a wave. The policeman nearest to him drew a pistol. Contreras gathered himself for the spring, crouching there like a great wild animal. I saw that this could easily end in tragedy so I pushed my way through to the policeman.

"Put up your gun, you barbarian!" I yelled in my most official tone. "Leave this to me."

In cases like this it is the most brazen person who wins.

The man may have taken me for one of his superiors; anyway, he obeyed. Then I turned to Contreras. "What's all this, Captain? Nobody here wants to hurt you."

"Better it is to hide behind a bush than to wait for prayers!" he growled in that stilted language of his.

"Come on out of there, Captain," I coaxed. "Don't let these people think you're afraid."

"If anyone thinks so," he said in a steely tone, "let the son of a whore come here!"

"Come on, come on, calm yourself!"

When Contreras finally climbed out and went along peaceably with me, there was a sparkle of satisfaction in Yuste's eyes. As for me, the applause I was giving inside for the way the whole scene had gone nearly deafened me.

From that day on all Madrid buzzed with talk. Excited crowds argued about Contreras as though the national security depended on his case. Then Yuste was disqualified from the College of Medicine and the excitement reached unexpected heights. The College refused to hear the doctor read his paper on the subject of indefinite catalepsy in general and the case of Alonso de Contreras in particular. This went against him although the majority of people, the masses, were clearly on our side. Then I wrote one of the most brilliant articles of my journalistic career. It was a diatribe against those people of all the ages who had refused to accept new discoveries in science and I dragged in everyone from Pasteur to Christopher Columbus.

God help us, what a row we'd started! Medical students rebelled against their teachers and the Youth Front threatened to lynch one of the doctors who had voted to expel Yuste. But this reaction of the public did not really solve our problems.

Yuste was humiliated and discouraged. He was actually on the point of fleeing from Madrid, leaving us holding the bag.

Then one day Contreras, doubled over with laughter, showed us a letter he had just received.

"By my sins! Read this letter, your lordships. I never knew there was a demand for such merchandise."

It seemed that the Department of Research of the Roosevelt University in New York was interested in acquiring possession of Contreras' body when he died, with the object of using it for intensive study.

Part of the contract stipulated that he live for at least three months of each year in the United States as guest of the University. They enclosed some money and said they would not object to advancing more, much more, provided the Captain insure himself with a recognized company in case, for any reason, Contreras' body could not be transported to the Research Center. Needless to say, we celebrated that day.

Now, several months later, dressing in front of the mirror, Contreras saw me smile.

"Why are you smiling? Are you making fun of my awkwardness?"

"No, no, I was just thinking about what we've been through."

"Well, enjoy yourself."

Contreras finished trimming his mustache, took off his dressing gown and began to look for his riding clothes. Every time I watched him dress I remembered the first time when, after his hair had been cut, his beard shaved and his mustache trimmed, he stood in front of the mirror and said triumphantly, "But I am young! Several centuries of sleep make one youthful!" Contreras was about fifty years old. With his gray beard and wild, straggling hair he had looked like a patriarch. Scissors and razor, vitamins and sunbaths soon made him a youthful handsome fifty, as dashing as a middle-aged motion picture star.

All during the time of the raging controversy around Yuste, I had kept the Captain more or less shut in. I was worried that people wouldn't yet recognize in him the fabulous man I had written about. What had to be done, I figured, was to adapt his habits, not to the manners of our day but to what people would expect of a man who had been a killer at twelve, a soldier at fourteen, a pirate at twenty, a monk at twenty-two, and a hunted criminal at twenty-seven; but who also, for most of his life, had been a charming courtier at a ducal court, a welcome guest in the house of the great writer Lope de Vega, and so on. At first I thought of having him be natural, letting him walk, speak, smile, eat, and act exactly as he did, but I quickly dismissed that idea, for being "natural" would have exposed him to sudden death every minute. His stare was so provoking, his roars of laughter so stentorian, his stride so exaggerated that he seemed more like a cari-

cature of himself than a true survivor of his era. So I
decided to smooth out the angles of his personality. This
had to be done in order to prepare the way for his future
exploitation, for all this was leading to one dream of
mine: one day Contreras would give lectures, lectures on
morals, theology, and love, lectures highly lucrative for
all of us.

During our stay in the Valley of Arán I worked out an
intensive cultural program for Captain Alonso. I not
only had to teach him the history of Spain from Philip
IV to our time, but also the political philosophical atmosphere of the present, the evolution of customs and ideas,
the progress of science, and the arts of war and navigation.

In Madrid, however, I undertook his social education.
This was harder, a lot harder. No one would have
thought so, but teaching him to walk was the most difficult. His natural way was to take long, slow strides, neck
stiff, head high, expression defiant, coupled with an odd
movement of the shoulders and an exaggerated swing of
the arms that was surprising and odd. I made him take
shorter steps, hold his neck less stiffly, and keep his
shoulders still.

Later, when he had practiced enough to go out, I had
to correct another defect deeply rooted in him. This was
the distrust with which he looked at passers-by. From the
time he spied them in the distance to the time they went
by he did not take his eyes off them. He would stare at
them half haughtily, half suspiciously. If they hesitated,
feeling themselves observed, Contreras would draw aside

as though to ward off an attack. If they were women he undressed them with his eyes. If they were ladies of quality he would stand aside fifteen feet before they reached him, and make what he considered a discreet bow.

At first everything about him was so extreme that his courtesy seemed servile, his show of friendship submissive, his unconformity a declaration of war. He ate with such gusto, always stuffing the fifth morsel into his mouth before swallowing the first, that he seemed to be making up for the three centuries he had fasted. He sawed with his elbows while he ate, and was almost always in a cheerful mood, merrily cursing Dr. Yuste for not letting him eat more than five courses, not counting soup and dessert. No sooner had he finished eating than he would flop into an armchair and take a nap as uninhibited as his eating; loud snores were interrupted by belches and other noises which made up in splendor what they lost in manners.

No. A "natural" Contreras would not have made attractive company.

Contreras' reactions were always primitive; they had the defect of being savage and the virtue of being simple. He lacked two very sophisticated qualities: malice and a sense of humor. The first was in his favor, but not the second. Loyalty, faith, absence of malice, generosity, were his characteristic virtues, while pride, boastfulness, impulsiveness, aggressiveness and suspicion constituted his essential defects. His distrust was completely innocent; it was the suspicion of the lamb that fears the wolf in disguise. It was easy to deceive Contreras. This made my work easier. He was not long in learning how to dress quickly, to smoke, to eat in moderation, to laugh without roaring, and to smile without menace.

The Captain had progressed admirably in manners; but he had acquired modern culture without assimilating it. That is to say, he knew what had happened since the beginning of his long sleep, but he could not help criticizing everything from the point of view of his first life. As to forms of thought and norms of conduct his attitude was indisputable, yet incompatible with ours. It was amazing how he could enter into some of the thoughts of a life so alien to him, and at the same time repudiate others. I finally realized that the essential difference between Contreras and a man of our age is that the Captain had instinctive mental scales for weighing values. His scales differed from ours in their positiveness as opposed to our negativeness. His classification of concepts was far different from ours. When a new idea or sensation came to him he instinctively classified and evaluated it according to his pre-established set of values of other things. My natural impatience as a superior modern man began to vanish before Contreras. I began to think that today our scales are out of order, that we no longer know the value of things, that we live in shadows, in the wind . . .

Cornejo, I had reprimanded myself, see that you mold the Captain, but don't let it be the Captain who molds you, or you'll probably end up the way he did, being a monk in Moncayo.

I came out of my reverie to see that now Contreras' face was clean and smooth and his rebellious hair combed back from the wide brow. The long, slow operation of bathing and dressing of a few months ago, he could now accomplish easily and quickly. Once his long legs were in riding breeches, his feet in military boots, and the cuffs of his shirt buttoned, he turned to the once complicated business of the necktie. But now he skillfully flipped it around his neck, crossed the ends, ran the knot, adjusted it carefully, and then looked at me for applause. I helped him into his hunting coat, and as he filled his pockets he recited the lesson he had learned: "In this pocket, the handkerchief, in this one, the wallet, the fountain pen here, the lighter and cigarette case, keys and coins here."

He paused doubtfully.

"You haven't forgotten anything," I said.

"No," he said, "but I miss my sword."

His insistence on buying a sword had disconcerted me. He did not want to use it — just as a sign of his station in life. "How does one distinguish a Knight now? — I am a Knight of Malta, but how does one know that? How do you even know a plain gentleman from one who is not?"

When I replied that one could usually tell a gentleman from his clothes he was perplexed, for that would mean that quality must be united to wealth, a thing which went against his ethics and reason.

Actually, however, in spite of this and other disquieting things, I could not complain of the Captain's progress. If his soul had remained virgin, his social form, the external manifestations of his character had advanced extraordinarily. And these were the minimal conditions for presenting the Captain to society.

I had struggled hard to reach the crossroads where we stood today. Contreras went down the front stairs ahead of me to where the car was waiting.

You don't know where you're going, I said to myself, but I know. Until that day his confinement and lessons had been solely directed toward making him "presentable." As yet he'd not been presented, but starting today Contreras would have to face society, face its art, its politics, its conventions, its prejudices, and its people — all kinds of people. How would he act in this world? How would the world act toward him?

I lagged behind, watching him go down the stairs, happy, confident and serene.

"Good luck to you, Captain," I breathed. "You'll need it."

CHAPTER FIVE

PACA REVILLA, even before her friendship with Contreras, was the most talked about woman in Madrid. Everything about her seemed designed to inspire talk: her beauty, her money, her wit, and her private life.

There was hardly ever a party given in Madrid that Paca wasn't invited to. But though everyone was delighted by her and laughed at her witty sallies, few bothered to defend her when the rumors would begin:

"My dear, have you heard what they say Paca Revilla's doing *now* . . ."

But she wasn't fazed when the latest gossip about herself was relayed to her. She'd make an amusing little *moue* which meant: You don't say, how very amusing, but I really don't give a damn.

Paca had crammed a lot into her few years — more than many women even read about in a lifetime. In her early teens she'd been in the midst of the Asturian Uprisings and had seen unbelievable atrocities committed on her parents' estate. When Spain's civil war broke out she was nineteen and just married. For three years before her marriage she'd had two serious suitors: one who loved her and one whom she loved. The first was the Count of Alcedo, the other Luis Seoane. Alcedo was extremely handsome and the better dancer; Luis was more refined, more intelligent and a brilliant conversationalist. She and Luis battled turbulently and frequently and several times they ended it all "forever and definitely" only to make up again passionately.

Alcedo took advantage of one of these quarrels to propose and was accepted. But she never was in love with him. Five months after the war started her husband's plane was shot down, and all she could feel inside was relief, relief that she was out of the unbearable sort of life that her false pride had got her into.

She never went into mourning, because at first Alcedo's death was not confirmed and she was afraid that widow's weeds would indicate a wish that it might be true. Then when her great love, Luis, died in battle also and the State confirmed Alcedo's death of the year before, Paca felt she could not go into mourning because gossiping tongues would certainly say she was mourning for her true love, Luis.

During the rest of the war Paca was a nurse at the front. After it was over she did not return to her parents' house in Asturias, but went back to the apartment she had lived in as a bride.

Paca was a woman of the world and she gave to the

world what it demanded of her: her personality, her smile, and her brittle wit. But she never gave her heart —or perhaps it had burned out.

Her world was not only the chic world of high society; she was often seen with journalists, artists, poets and matadors. She was anything but a snob, and this was partly responsible for the rumors about her. My dear, one saw her with the oddest people! Among the "odd people" was me.

Paca was at the height of her beauty when she met Captain Contreras, but she was far from just a fashion plate. She was cultivated; she was like a gem that the jeweler had worked on with special care so that it gleamed in all its facets. She was gay, frank, witty, sophisticated, and incurably fond of novelty.

If one had to find a fault in her there were two: a touch of cynicism and the secret of knowing how to close her heart against anything remotely akin to love or any other emotion which might ultimately cause her pain.

Two days before Alonso de Contreras had been putting on his riding breeches in front of the mirror, I'd gone to Paca and asked her to help me launch him in society. She was enthusiastic and promised her co-operation. She had a reason to be enthusiastic. Contreras, who had not been seen in public since his arrival in handcuffs at the station, was still the chief topic of conversation, of sermons, and of the newspapers.

"Naturally, darling, I'm dying to meet the man," Paca told me, "but first I want the truth about him. Who is he, *really?*"

"Paca, I swear that this man is the authentic Captain Contreras. You know I wouldn't fool you."

She smiled and patted my hand condescendingly. "All right, I believe you."

"But I swear by all that's holy, the whole thing is true — I didn't believe it myself at first, but wait till you meet him."

"I can hardly wait. We'll launch him in great style."

Sure enough, she telephoned us shortly after that to invite us to a hunt on the estate of some friends near Avila. It was to be an eagle shoot, and I was sure that Contreras would like it and that he would be a good hunter. I said she called us, but it was really Contreras she called. He was half dressed when I handed him the telephone. It was the first time he'd used one except in make-believe. He could not understand how a woman's voice could sound like that, and he kept taking the receiver away from his ear and looking at it as though he expected her to step out of it, shrunken to the size of her voice.

"Answer her!" I whispered. "Say something!"

"I can't — I'm naked!" he answered, completely bewildered; if he could hear her she could see him. I had to take the telephone away from him to find out what she wanted.

Contreras' reaction to the instrument was both comic and disconcerting. Neither aviation (he swore there'd been inventors working on flying in his day) nor the atomic bomb (just one more explosion) nor the radio (a perfected music box) had impressed him like the telephone and the automobile. His next admiration was for running water (those little rivers that spurt out of the walls) and electric light bulbs (pieces of imprisoned sun).

We went to the country in an open convertible driven by Paca. When I introduced them poor Contreras' eyes were immediately magnetized by hers. The first minute we were alone he declared: "This is the most perfect woman God has formed — she is like a miracle!"

As for her, before we got into the car she managed to whisper, "Your Captain is *very* attractive."

We started off, and Contreras seemed to become modernized by the sensation of speed. To his wonderment, Paca turned on the radio. He burst out delightedly: "I swear by my black sins that everything is better nowadays! Man has made life beautiful."

"And woman?" asked Paca. "Don't you think, Captain, that she also contributes to its beauty?"

Contreras became thoughtful and he took his time to answer.

"To say that she contributes to the beauty of life is rather narrow, señora," he said in his archaic but pleasant accent. "The stars are the magnets of the night. The sun is the painter of nature. Water is the comfort of the earth. But at the same time, the stars may trick the navigator, the sun can burn planets, and water can drown the earth. And in the same way woman, who is the fountain and prime motivation of our sadness or happiness, is to life like the stars, or the sun or the water."

Paca was a little disconcerted by this reply to her small talk, but she managed a gay laugh.

"Bravo!" she said. "I'm glad that we are so important."

We got to the estate of the Count and Countess of Robledo at one o'clock. The guests were having drinks in the garden. They were all chattering excitedly, and I assumed it was about us, for as soon as we arrived they stopped.

The owner of the estate, a man of seventy, affable and crafty, stood up when he saw us. He introduced us to his wife, a still handsome woman and one that was more observing than suited me; she studied us with so much curiosity that I began to develop a necktie complex and thought perhaps I had overdone the hunting designs in mine.

With them there was a Sweet Young Thing, Dorita Rivas, very smiling, very well groomed, very modern, and very much a type. Also an intelligent-looking man with big ears — named Morales — who I at first took to be the manager of the estate, but who later turned out, rather disconcertingly I was to find, to be with the police. Then the chaplain, neat and circumspect, and the black-market oil magnate, Cosme Molludo, with two diamond rings on his big hands; and finally a diplomat whose name I won't mention because you'd know it. The last two were the only ones I even knew by sight. The diplomat, polished and honeyed, was rather popular in Madrid, people not being quite sure whether to admire him more for his arrogance or his ignorance.

I was relieved to see Contreras greet everyone fairly correctly. He kissed all the ladies' hands, bending over almost at right angles. He shook the men's hands firmly, so firmly that, though I'd warned him, some of the men, the diplomat in particular, nursed their sore fingers afterwards.

Once he'd said "How do you do?" to everyone he did not know what to say and would not move a step away from me. They all looked him up and down quite rudely, and he started to get nervous. He put his weight on one foot and then the other, like an actor in his first play.

"So you're the famous Captain Contreras?" our hostess said at last, breaking the silence.

"To serve your ladyship, the Countess!" he answered much too grandly, clicking his heels.

The Sweet Young Thing smothered a giggle, and I became as upset as if he'd been my son and just come out with a swear word.

There was another silence. Everyone was trying to think of something to say. Finally they all seemed to begin to talk at once, saying whatever came into their silly heads, nervousness making their questions unusually rude and stupid.

"You're very handsome, Captain."

"Do you know how to fence?"

"Are you a bachelor?"

"How old are you — I mean, really, *exactly* how old are you?"

"Is *everything* the newspapers say about you true?"

I noticed with horror that the Captain's face was getting red and that any moment he was going to erupt. I tried to say something but it was too late.

"Have I been invited to a hunt or called before the tribunal?" he bellowed suddenly.

A third silence longer than the others. Count Robledo
turned away uncomfortably. His wife acquired a nervous
tic and wrinkled her nose. The Sweet Young Thing was
importunate enough to begin again.

"Now don't be naughty, Captain. You know, we're
dying to hear what you have to say. After all, we've heard
so much about you. You still haven't said whether you're
married or a bachelor."

Paca began to cough nervously, but I knew she was
really enjoying this. I hurriedly started to talk about the
latest soccer match in Madrid but Contreras interrupted.

"I am a widower, my lady," he said with steely calm-
ness to the girl, "I killed my wife because she went to
bed with a friend of mine — what else would you like
to know?"

Dorita Rivas blushed deeply. The Countess' tic got
worse. The Count turned pale. The diplomat mumbled
something. Contreras looked at them all challengingly.

"Ask me, ask me! I shall satisfy you all. I always
satisfy people who pry into the lives of others. Why does
the lady blush? To the blazing fires of hell with such
delicacy!"

Any more of this and I'd have quietly passed out. But
Paca leapt into the breach and started to talk about the
hunt. She asked if there were many eagles this year and
on which part of the mountain our blinds were to be and
so on. Everybody rushed into the conversation, some saying there'd never been so many eagles, others saying not
one had been seen this year. Contreras listened to this
for a while, then he slumped down in a chair. The lunch
was late being served, and the talk about eagles more pro-

longed than the subject warranted, so Contreras began to yawn conspicuously. Our hostess watched him nervously out of the corner of her eye, but he, the beast, would not stop yawning.

This was Captain Contreras' introduction to high society.

CHAPTER SIX

AFTER LUNCH some of the guests went off to take siestas while the rest of us got ready for the shoot. Contreras, Paca and I made a group with Morales, the police official, the chaplain, the Sweet Young Thing and our host. To try out this new weapon known as a shotgun, Contreras shot a lark perched in a tree.

"No, you meany," squealed Dorita Rivas. "People just don't shoot sitting birds!"

"It's one of the hunters' rules," agreed the chaplain pontifically.

Contreras glanced at them but didn't answer.

We reached our chosen spot where a boy was waiting for us with a "grand duke" on a chain. This is the Castilian name for one of the fiercest birds of prey, the giant owl. The chaplain told us that the owl spent his nights preying on the nests of other birds. He was so cruel and rapacious that all the other birds were in league against him and hunted him by day when he was blind.

The boy tied the grand duke by one foot to a stake in the ground. We went into a blind covered with pine boughs to hide from the sharp eyes of the eagles. Perched on the stake the owl was so quiet that he looked stuffed. Soon, though, he began to beat his wings as though sensing danger. A block of magpies began screaming; they swooped over him, then flew off into the distance.

"They've gone to tell the eagles," the chaplain said eagerly, "so that they'll come and kill him."

Contreras was sitting on the ground between Paca and the Sweet Young Thing. Dorita was apologizing for having called the Captain a meany. She chattered on about how she really hadn't meant it as an insult because she rather liked men who were, you know, brutes. Her fiancé had been so proper and formal, and everyone said how admirable he was that she couldn't stand it and had broken the engagement.

"Don't talk so much," said our host, "you'll scare off the eagles."

The grand duke opened his wings and hopped from the stake to the ground. He was trembling and turning his head from side to side, looking uneasily into the sky with his great blind eyes. His beak was half open ready to defend himself against an invisible enemy. Suddenly he calmed down again and jumped up on the stake to resume his pose.

"Some prisoners are like that," Morales said reflectively. "They pass from almost childish terror to absolute indifference."

"It's curious to observe," said the Count, "that the

grand duke is more frightened when he merely *senses* the eagles than when they actually attack him."

"Like all criminals," Morales added cheerfully. "Unfortunately, I've had to witness several executions and I've noticed that most of the condemned go to the gallows more calmly than when threatened with the third degree."

The owl hopped to the ground again in a sudden panic. He tried to break his chain with his beak. He tried to fly, his body quivering and his head and neck feathers ruffled.

"There are the eagles!"

They were circling very high, majestic and serene, as though they knew they were the lords of the air. The cowardly magpies, still screaming, followed them at a discreet distance. The eagles circled lower, satellites of an invisible planet. Suddenly one of them extended his talons, lowered his head, and plunged straight down at the motionless owl. The eagle grazed the ground, and, without landing, jabbed out at the owl with his great beak, and then soared up again slowly.

Our host did not shoot, so as to give his guests the first shot, but we were too absorbed by the spectacle to raise our guns. Then another eagle swooped down and Paca let him have both barrels, and it fell to earth leaving a trail of feathers. The one behind him tried to gain altitude but was shot down also.

Then suddenly there was a cry.

"Hey, don't shoot!" shouted the diplomat, appearing around a hill. "It's I!"

"Now what does *he* want?" asked our host.

"He's heard that we're entertaining a grand duke," said Paca, "and he wants to be introduced."

We all chuckled except Contreras, who was still a little suspicious of humor. We started back for the house. A boy carried the dead eagles, another one brought back the grand duke, who'd been rewarded with two live lizards.

After supper the diplomat suggested that we play that game where one asks the same questions of everybody and then tries to analyze him by his answers. He began with an innocent one: "Which landscape is nearest to your heart?"

Dorita, who'd never been there, thought it'd be elegant to say "Paris." Paca, with more simplicity than her young friend, said, "The sea." The diplomat said coyly and unblushingly that his favorite landscape was the one reflected in a woman's eyes. Contreras, his eyes cloudy with memories, said, "The hills of Moncayo."

The second question was a bit more intimate. "What was your worst mistake, your worst sin, or the thing you regret most having done?"

The diplomat: "Not having known at twenty-five what I know now." Dorita (blushing): "I can't tell you!" Paca: "I regret having done things I haven't gotten the credit for, and not having done all the things they say I have." Morales: "I regret some occasions when I've had to do my duty even though it pained me." Contreras (troubled and moved at the memory): "Not having given a man and a woman I killed in Palermo time to repent their sins."

The next question ended the game. "What act in your life gave you the most satisfaction?"

"In some ways, all of them," said the diplomat, with a modest lowering of his head.

"In some ways none of them," said Paca.

"The thing that pleases me most is whatever project is at hand," said Morales.

Everyone turned to look at Contreras expectantly.

"What pleases me most," he said slowly, "is having cast off a bad Christian on a desert island, naked and without food so that he might purge himself from sin by dying of hunger."

"*This* I'll have to hear more about!" exclaimed Paca.

The game could not go on. They wanted to hear Contreras. He had dropped three murders as casually as though he were offering us cigarettes. Perhaps some of his listeners thought that Contreras had chosen this occasion to hold the floor, but I knew that nothing was farther from his heart. He was incapable of understanding the nuances of the game; he took it seriously, not realizing that he was expected to lie a bit and that if this weren't true the other players would have confessed far worse things than they did. He'd refused, against all entreaty, to tell us more about the couple in Palermo, but was quite willing to tell us in detail about what had pleased him most.

He was at that time in command of a frigate whose purpose was to spy out the movements of the Turkish Armada, warn the cities that were in danger and take arms against the infidel. One day on an island called Astypalea, near Rhodes, he was told that a Christian frigate had abducted the Patriarch of the island and was holding him for ransom. Contreras was angry that there could be Christians in Turkish waters so wicked as to rob other Christians, so he readied his ship for battle and went looking for the corsair. He found and took him without bloodshed. He asked to see the corsair's papers of authorization from the Viceroy and saw that they were false. He took him prisoner, returned the Patriarch to his island, and cast off the corsair on a desert island, naked and without food.

"As death by hunger is slow," he concluded, "he had plenty of time to repent his sins."

"And you left him to die of hunger?" the diplomat asked, quite shocked.

"The Greeks on the Island of Astypalea begged me to forgive him, but I told them not to anger me, for that was the way to punish hostile Christians."

"If your reasons convinced those Greeks," sniffed the diplomat, "then they were as bad as you."

"They weren't wicked at all," said Contreras. "On the contrary, they were very polite and hospitable. They wanted me to marry the Governor's daughter and the women gave me so many kisses that I can still feel them."

"Were they pretty?" someone asked.

He shrugged. "All kinds, as in every other place, in the world. They wore skirts to the middle of the leg, colored jackets, and scarlet silk petticoats. And pearls on their foreheads, and open-toed slippers."

"Just like today!" said Dorita with interest.

Morales acted like a motor that was always in gear, a

low gear, but always in operation. He wore a constant cynical smile as Contreras talked, as though he were looking for a trap, a trick, in the Captain's story. I didn't like it. He made me uncomfortable.

Contreras, recalling the beauty of the Governor's daughter, ended his tale, sighing, "If I had wanted to enjoy myself on her body no one would have stopped me."

The Sweet Young Thing had a slight coughing attack and they had to bring her water. Morales and I stared at some etchings over the mantelpiece. The diplomat, shocked, said good night to the ladies and went to his room.

But while Contreras talked Paca listened to him intently, as though able (and she was) to listen to him while following her own thoughts. She listened with a sort of admiring tenderness, and when he finished she was silent, as though her thoughts were continuing where he had left off.

That night could have brought about a terrible scandal. Paca, Dorita, Contreras and I went for a stroll before going to our rooms. There was a moon, and the country was full of the little sounds, crickets, cicadas, nocturnal wing-flutters, that come in the silence of Castilian nights. Paca and I stayed behind Contreras and Dorita who had gone on ahead. We couldn't see them but could hear their voices.

"Listen," said Paca, "are you in any sort of mess with the Police?"

"No."

"Well, look out for Morales. I get the feeling that he's trying to pin something on you."

I shrugged.

Then we heard Dorita's voice: "Leave me alone, you brute, leave me alone!"

And Contreras: "I don't give back what has been given to me!"

"Go see what's happening," said Paca, startled.

But suddenly Dorita came running toward us.

"He's — He's a monster! I don't know what he wants of me, but he's a beast." She showed us red wrists. "He hurt me!"

"Did you kiss him?" asked Paca coolly.

"Well, yes, of course."

"What do you mean, 'of course'? Stupid! when you don't know the rules you shouldn't play the game."

Contreras appeared, coming toward us. Dorita ran off, and Paca followed her. Contreras looked furious. This was a trick! A trap! She had called him handsome, had leaned up against him, and told him that some women knew how to kiss better than they did on Astypalea.

I tried to calm him. I told him that what he'd tried to do was not only taking too much for granted but also slightly barbarous and ungentlemanly. He leaped at me, took me by the lapels and sent me sprawling to the ground with a violent shove. Then he put his right hand automatically to his hip for his sword, and not finding it stood waiting for me to return his attack — which I had no intention of doing, I can assure you. Finally his expression became calmer. Then he thrust out his big hand

and growled in what was for him a conciliatory tone: "Get up, Mr. Scribbler, and let us go to bed!"

"The next lesson," I said ruefully, accepting his hand, "will be on the subject of *nuance* — "

"The next lessons," he snapped back, "will be given by *me*."

CHAPTER SEVEN

ALL THAT TIME Contreras was enjoying a process of what, for lack of a better word, I'll call bedazzlement. He thought everything he saw was better than in his first life; easier, more comfortable, happier. And the more things dazzled him the higher he climbed that peak from which he was to fall.

But we shall not anticipate events. We are at the moment of Contreras' initial delight with his new world. Suddenly he was rich and overwhelmed with attention. Spain was at the height of an inflation which gave everyone a marvelous feeling of false well-being. The banks gave credit, the market went up, great fortunes were made. I began to build Contreras a house, so we sold all our stocks for a high price. Our brokers sold them to others even higher, and who knows to whom they were sold the highest.

Paca Revilla went with Contreras to museums, factories and hospitals. She took him to opening nights at the theater and to concerts. She introduced him to her circle of poets and painters. She took him to the bull-fights, and even managed to have him invited to scientific research centers. They would take her car for what was to be a day's excursion, but Contreras would become so intoxicated by speed that he would refuse to come back. Paca would give in and they would be away for three weeks. Contreras was continually expanding his mental horizons by living in the best hotels, visiting shipyards and watching ships launched, by speaking with navy cap-tains on board cruisers, by submerging in a submarine, and by flights in military planes.

When Paca and Contreras left Madrid they always managed to come back by the coast, no matter how far out of the way it was. Contreras insisted on this. It delighted him to cover in a few hours what he'd covered by ship or on foot or by mule, taking days, weeks or months.

"Spain has shrunk," he would say. Of our three seas his favorite was the Mediterranean because of its long history of invasions, and because of what it had brought from the Orient: commerce, glass, purple, the alphabet, and art. They used to stop the car on the shore toward evening, and she would encourage him to tell her tales of his adventures. She did not really believe in him, you understand; not yet. She still thought of him as mine and Yuste's, but *not* the real Contreras. But she enjoyed listening to his stories no matter who he was.

"How good you smell!" he exclaimed one day. "Now I know that if by a miracle I were to return to my first world I could not live in it." And he told her of how one day when he was riding in the subway he smelled a strong odor near him. That smell transported him centuries back to the woman he loved, Isabel, for whom he had killed his Captain. He turned eagerly and found a filthy woman next to him; she was uncombed, blear-eyed, and she stank. He was startled that the smell of this beggar woman should have reminded him of Isabel. And then the realization came to him that the sweaty woman-smell, like a sheep or a mare, was the smell peculiar to the women of his era.

"Didn't they use perfumes?"

"Yes, they used civet and amber and pomander, but their odors were stronger, so that when the scent wore off, the odors were stronger than ever. They didn't wash. Now every time I smell a bad odor I think of those days. Even though they did not repel me then, I think now that the houses must have smelled like dead bodies, and people like cattle, streets like excrement, and barracks and universities like urine and sweat."

"How very unattractive it must have been."

"Not really, because then I knew no better. It's only now that I see the difference — all the running water, sewers and drains, and above all, a bath with soap — it's so much pleasanter to live now."

When he came back from one of these excursions he said to me, "I want to see everything. I want to learn everything. Some things still elude me: men and women. Look how much they have accomplished. And yet, when I try to get to the bottom of them and find out the ultimate reason for their being, I perceive a lack of self-confidence in them, as though they wanted to keep the secret of progress and success to themselves."

"Perhaps you're looking for something in them that isn't there."

He looked at me a long time.

"It can't be, it just can't be!" he said at last. "See what man has done." He opened the windows wide and looked out over the clean, orderly, powerful city. "This did not appear by itself. It is man who has done it."

One afternoon he put on a strange scene. He said of it later, "It was not only I who was speaking, but all my ancestors."

According to Paca Revilla it had been an extraordinary experience. They had driven up Mount Tibidabo, and Contreras was completely enraptured by the view of Barcelona. It was late afternoon, and the great ships were steaming out of the harbor. The breeze blew against their faces. One by one the lights went on in the city, and the cobwebs of the streets were traced out with strings of lights. The great blue shadows of buildings burst into needles of light as though reflecting the sky's stars. Contreras began to breathe quickly. Suddenly he took his arm from around her waist, went forward a few steps, and began to declaim in a loud voice.

"Great God! Great God! How I delight in Your magnificence and in that of Your children! It is plain to see that they were made in Your image, for see what they have done!"

Paca was stupefied. She tugged at his jacket and told

him to be quiet, that people were looking at him. He did not hear her.

"Great God, You made man out of perishable clay, but You breathed an immortal soul into him with intelligence and memory and free will. You expelled him from Paradise that he might create his own with the means You gave him. And he has done so, Great God! He has discovered the secrets of nature and the forces You have hidden in the air, in the waters and in the cosmic dust of the stars. You have guided him so that we all delight in Your generosity. Man has gone slowly, Great God of Sinai, limping and twisting, but at last he has come to what You wanted of him, You Who are the Way and the Truth and the Life!"

Contreras had his arms raised in the shape of a V, like a St. John by El Greco. His eyes flashed with emotion. At this point Paca turned and went back to the car; a group of curious onlookers took her place, circling about Contreras with open mouths.

He went on: "How it delights me to see how Your creatures have fulfilled their destiny! You too, oh children of God, sing praises to God our Lord. But what am I saying? You praise Him with Your factories, Davids in cement, with the sweet lauds of Your machines. What better psalm than the song of your motors! What better dance than the motion of your wheels and cylinders in homage to the Lord, even as the Dance of the Seises in the Cathedral of Sevilla who dance with castanets before the High Altar!"

Some whispered that he must be the prophet foretold by Mother Ráfols.

"He's an escaped lunatic," said others, and laughed uneasily.

"Maybe he's the Anti-Christ."

He stopped as suddenly as he'd begun and strode to the car.

After he got in, Paca did not start the motor at once. She was pale. He said nothing. Then she drove away quickly. As soon as they had passed the people, however, she stopped the car and turned to him.

"Who are you?" she whispered.

Contreras did not answer.

"Today, for the first time, I don't believe you are a lie. Cornejo could never have taught you what you just said. Are you really what you say you are? Who are you?"

Paca had turned off the lights. The top of the car was down. The high heaven was pierced by stars.

"Look," said Contreras, "see how the stars speak to me? They are like a flagship signaling her fleet, and every flag has a meaning. I have lost my flagship, lost the North Star, and I am waiting for the signal. The stars are sending me signals, now, but I do not know their code."

Contreras rested his head on her shoulder.

"If I did not feel your breathing beside me, or your heartbeats, I, Captain Contreras, would be afraid."

And Paca lowered her gaze from the sky where the stars went on winking tirelessly.

From that day on, Paca Revilla began to limit her outings with Contreras. There were no more excursions. Sometimes she'd say she was sick; other times she begged me to go with them because she didn't want to be alone with him.

She tried to justify her attitude to me by saying that the more she became convinced of Contreras' authenticity the less she wanted to be with him; it gave her "an indescribable fear of losing her mind." I didn't believe her for a moment. The truth was that she was afraid of falling in love, and she was fleeing from him just as she had fled from anyone else who began to disturb her. Soon she announced that she was going on a trip. She said that some English friends had invited her on a Mediterranean cruise, and that she would be gone for several months. "I shall gaze often at the stars," she wrote in her farewell letter to Contreras, "to see if they will give me a message from you. Nothing could please me more than to act as messenger from your flagship."

Contreras was very depressed over Paca's flight and I refrained from telling him that her trip was an excuse for not seeing him.

"Have you said anything about love to her?" I asked the Captain cautiously, for you never knew how he was going to take something like this.

"No," he answered.

"And how about her — has she?"

"Often, but only joking. If I try to get serious she always changes the subject right away."

"So you're not in love — "

"To the very depths of me. But I don't tell her — I'm so afraid of losing her."

And he became as sad as a lovesick student.

CHAPTER EIGHT

The commotion produced by Contreras' appearance
in the Almudena Cemetery would have died down in a
few months if I hadn't known the exact doses of news
about him to measure out to the press. If Contreras had
gone from the cemetery to a quiet flat on Calle de La-
gasca, nobody would remember him today, just as nobody
remembers dozens of truly extraordinary people who silently sink into oblivion because they don't have a good
press agent.

But in the case of Contreras the interest, the discussions, the articles and the bets did not slow down one bit.
I damn well saw to it that they didn't. The whole country became divided into pro and con factions about him
with the pros gaining. Sometimes in the beginning we
had to change houses or sleep in hotels, for on returning
to our own flat we'd find a crowd waiting for us. But
when Contreras began to go out into the world and peo-

ple would hear that he'd been to a cocktail party here or a hunt there, the hostesses would be driven mad the next day by telephone calls, mostly from complete strangers, who wanted details about his personality or to find out if such-and-such an anecdote about him were true.

And the rumors, good God! Such as the absolutely false one about his having had a violent fight with the Mayor of Madrid over some difference of opinion.

One of the incidents I didn't write about at the time, since it might have got me unpleasantly involved, was the visit to Dr. Yuste by some German officers accompanied by a doctor of the same nationality and a representative from their Embassy. Dr. Yuste sent them on to me. They were very polite and most interested in the process employed by Valenzuela and Luigi which had so prolonged Contreras' life. The German doctor had been working for years along similar lines, more ambitious ones than those of the famous Dr. Voronoff, whose object had been to double man's lifespan, so naturally he was most anxious to learn Valenzuela's process. He knew, of course, that it was possible to induce a cataleptic state of long duration. The Hindu fakirs, for example, were able to keep themselves apparently dead for forty days. Why not for forty years, or four hundred years?

It was absolutely imperative that he have the formula. He was on the verge of discovering it himself, he only needed a little more research . . .

We did not have the formula, only the live results. The doctor wished to meet Contreras so I sent for him, and he explained what he could. The doctor examined

his gums, his nose, and gave special attention to his eyelids and nails. While studying him he gave several exclamations in German which I did not understand, but
which caused excitement among the officers and the Embassy man. When he finished he took Contreras by the
shoulders and gave him an enthusiastic kiss on the cheek.

(Now that the World War is over and Der Führer vanished from the ruins of his Chancellery, I often wonder
when people discuss Hitler's being alive or not whether
that doctor managed to discover the formula in time.)

We used to go to see Yuste periodically. He would ask
us various routine questions and then chase us out at the
end of half an hour so that he might get on with his
work. He seemed to be getting more and more strange.
He rarely called us, and then only to analyze pieces of
Contreras' skin, or to make some special test.

The last few times he'd acquired the unpleasant habit
of not addressing me at all. He would go to Contreras
and take him by the shoulders.

"This is it, my boy," he'd say cryptically, "this is it."
Or "You'll soon be a man. Until now you have been only
a shadow."

One day he wouldn't even open the door, but called
out hoarsely: "Go along, boy, go along and come back
next week. I'll have something good for you."

After the war ended we packed our bags, arranged our
affairs and flew to the United States to fulfill our contract
with Roosevelt University.

It wasn't easy to get a passport for Contreras since
officially he didn't exist. Three times our applications

were refused. When I saw that nothing was to be done through regular channels I went to an influential brother of mine and got him to ask me to dinner with one of the officials in charge of these matters. We received the passport without any trouble. Dr. Yuste thought of offering him money, but it wasn't necessary. In Spain one does not influence with money but with friendship. (In contrast to the United States where my personal charms were far less useful than Alonso's money!)

One evening, shortly after we'd arrived in New York, we decided to dine at the terrace grill of the hotel we were staying at. Contreras, in a dinner jacket, was trying not to look quite so obviously agonized in the stiff collar. He couldn't get used to it, nor to the rapid elevators. We zoomed up the eighty floors toward the terrace, and in the small space of the elevator the packed-in people were silent. Contreras stared weakly at floor numbers flashing on and off, and didn't breathe until we got to the top and stepped out. We went into the dining room hoping for a good table near the orchestra, and the maître d'hôtel bustled up and said in perfect Spanish, "Señor Cornejo, Señor Contreras, will you follow me, please?"

"What's this?" I asked.

"A lady would like you to dine at her table. This way, please."

Seated at her table, more beautiful than ever, and smiling as we approached, was Paca Revilla.

CHAPTER NINE

THE CAPTAIN'S suite, next to the one I occupied with Dr. Yuste, consisted of a large sitting room, a medium-sized terrace, a small bedroom, a minute bathroom and a microscopic kitchen.

The sitting room, with its engravings of horses and dogs, a built-in bar which lit up when you opened it, a magnificent Dalton urn, its radio disguised as a bookcase, and its comfortable leather armchairs, was very English; comfort predominated over luxury. The terrace, on the other hand, with vines climbing up its painted walls, its marble shells hiding the indirect light to the ceiling, its small blue fishpond, its white-painted iron railing and its glass table and chairs, was very American; comfort supplanted by theatrical scenery. The sitting room was elegant without being pretentious. The terrace tried to be elegant without succeeding.

Contreras, in a white dinner jacket, with a silk handkerchief in his breast pocket and a cigarette in his mouth, glanced from the clock to the mirror. Seeing his reflection, he had to smile.

"Oh, Captain Contreras, how many have seen you," he said, "and who sees you now?"

When, in his first life, he had realized that Valenzuela, who held him bound and a prisoner, was a Moor, he'd wanted to escape, thinking it better to die on the gibbet than to play at ninepins with Satan throughout eternity. He used to imagine himself in hell with his Christian face, but dressed in the costume of a Moor or a renegade, a turban on his head, slippers on his feet and a scimitar in his belt. That disguise would be the INRI the demons had put there for being a traitor to his race and his faith. And this other disguise he saw himself wearing now, was it also that of a renegade?

Was he not in a land of heretics, receiving money from the hands of Calvinists and Lutherans who shared their cloaks and their bread with him even as Lope de Vega had done before them? "With men like you one must share one's cloak," he remembered Lope's words wistfully.

"Oh, Captain Contreras, how many have seen you, and who sees you now? Near these very waters you helped defeat Sir Walter Raleigh — you defeated him to save Puerto Rico which he had surrounded.

"Of what use was your victory? Now . . . after centuries . . . Walter Raleigh has taken Puerto Rico. In the Governor's Palace they speak only English."

Contreras passed a hand over his brow, closing and

locking the door of his memory just as he had done that day — so near and yet so long ago! — outside of Toledo.

Contreras turned on the radio, lowered the lights and poured himself a Scotch. Paca Revilla would be there soon.

During the ten days she had been in New York they had seen each other every night except for three on which the laboratory sessions at the University had lasted longer than usual, and one on which Contreras had been half dazed from being hypnotized and subjected to the lie detector.

Paca and he used to go to Fornos, the Spanish restaurant on Fifty-second Street, or to little French or Italian restaurants. Then they would go dancing until they closed the place. (I had seen to it, of course, that Alonso had taken dancing lessons and though his style always remained vaguely archaic, he had the great natural rhythm and agility of a swordsman.) Contreras was amazed that Paca, always so reserved when they were alone, should dance with him cheek to cheek in public. These conventions, the Captain told himself, even the wise man Merlin would not have been able to understand.

Good Lord, hadn't she told him she'd missed him terribly, hadn't she showed up here in New York to be with him? Hadn't she said she couldn't stay away from him?

"That means — " he'd started eagerly.

"That does *not* mean that you should become serious."

"But why . . ."

"Men who become serious about love," said Paca

lightly, "develop fish-faces. Everybody has the face of an animal — look, that one is an owl, that one a rooster, and that one a mouse, and I don't mind tiger-faces or bear-faces or bull-dog-faces, but fish-faces! Fish-faces shatter me. Fish are so sad!"

But tonight — tonight would be different — it had to be different! For this morning she'd said out of the blue, "Do you realize we've been seeing each other all this time and I still haven't seen your rooms? Why don't you ask me to supper, just the two of us?"

Now Contreras straightened his tie in front of the mirror, and looked impatiently at the clock. Supposing she didn't show up?

When she finally arrived the sitting room was dark except for the dim light of the bar and a blaze of light from the terrace. From the bookcase languid music floated in velvety tones. Paca gave a laugh then said, "I'm sorry, Alonso, it's just that it looks like a moving picture set!"

Contreras apologized. She would have to excuse him if anything was wrong. This was the first time he'd done anything like this. He had placed himself in the hands of the maître d'hôtel who had arranged it all, the lighting effects, the music, even the menu. Paca objected only to the lights. She did not like them so dim. She poured herself a drink of whiskey and offered one to him. A little later they had dinner on the terrace, sitting across from each other. Contreras was careful about every detail of etiquette, and Paca praised him.

"You've become a great gentleman."

"I never was but I always wanted to be. When I was

in the service of the Count and Countess of Monterrey the Countess used to laugh when I told her I wanted to be a rich nobleman when I was old. Have a house and property, spend my time between taking care of my estate, hunting and reading. I have read little, but now I should like to."

Paca sipped her champagne slowly, looking at Contreras over her glass.

"Alonso," she said hesitantly, "one day I asked you who you were. You told me who you thought you were — "

"Not who I thought I was," he said calmly, "who I knew I was."

"But are you sure that everything you see, everything you think, is really the way things are?"

"I don't understand philosophy, Paca. I know who I am, what I am, how I am."

"And you've never wondered if all this isn't a dream? Have you never thought that you yourself, Contreras, might be a dream?"

"No, Paca, I see that I really and truly exist; that there is a God who created me; that there are other creations around me: stones, flowers, animals, men, created by the same God. I see that man, who in his early ages was like a beast except that he had a soul, has gone on progressing, thanks to the divine breath which that soul enclosed, till today when everything is better than yesterday."

She was silent a moment. "Sometimes I think that everything around us is a lie. And the worst lie is man's progress which seems to dazzle you so much."

He made a gesture of displeasure. Paca added with

great tenderness in her eyes: "But of all the lies that surround us I like yours the best."

"What do you mean?" he exclaimed. "Is all this a lie too?"

He stood up and went up to the balustrade, waving a hand at the city below. Paca joined him.

"Is this a lie?" he repeated.

Paca did not reply.

He went on: "Everything that we see from here, the great buildings, the lights, the power, proves that if today's man did all this, and the man of my day did not, the man of today is better."

"And do you believe," Paca interrupted, "that man has progressed in spirit, in faith, in love for his neighbor, in justice, as much as he has in chemistry, and mechanics, and organization?"

"One must suppose that he has."

"And what if one of these days you suddenly realize you're wrong?"

"I would think that the world had gone lame."

"Well, start convincing yourself, Captain Contreras. It's lame, all right — lame and without crutches."

They were silent a long time. The lighted advertisements on the buildings blinked on and off in changing colors. From the distant street rose a great sea of sound in which the distinct noises which formed it were lost like isolated drops; but on its surface waves of individual noise were heard from time to time: a train's whistle, the sea-cow moo of a liner coming into the harbor, the honking of horns in a traffic jam.

At last Paca moved away from the balustrade and went inside. "The world has epilepsy. And this is the heart of the world! Of *our* world, Captain Contreras!"

Contreras followed her. He was upset. He felt in some way to blame that the world displeased Paca. It was the fault of the terrace. It was the maître d'hôtel's fault, and the wine's, too. In his day when one wished to make love to a woman one did not need the artificial collaboration of liquor. And he had invited Paca here to make love to her, not to talk philosophy.

"Adiós, Contreras," Paca said suddenly, holding out her hand. "It's late."

Alonso felt the floor start to give way beneath him. He felt as deceived as he had with Dorita Rivas the night after the eagle hunt. It seemed obvious that if Paca had accepted the invitation to his suite, it was not to dine and discuss New York. Contreras grasped her hand.

"You're not going."

She made no move to free her hand, but she looked at him so coldly that he let her go.

"No!" she said sharply. Then, softening her tone, "Goodbye, Contreras. Tomorrow we shall see each other again. Tomorrow's the dinner in honor of Dr. Yuste, isn't it?" She smiled and went out of the door. She had scarcely closed it behind her when there was a tremendous crash in the room. Contreras had picked up the Dalton urn and smashed it against the floor. Paca came back, closing the door behind her.

"Are you crazy?" she said. "What short of childishness is this?"

He caught her in his arms, yanked her to him, and kissed her fiercely.

She made no move to resist. When he let her go she moved back a step, breathing hard. She tossed her head as though she were trying to shake off a disturbing thought. Then she recovered herself and taking him by the hand, she led him to the sofa and sat down beside him.

"You haven't any common sense, Captain Contreras. Hush now and listen to me, something you've not done before. Listen to me even though I'm afraid we're not going to understand each other."

Paca explained that she was too interested in Alonso to risk something that would spoil their friendship. She said she knew love only as a cruel and fickle god who required a regular sacrifice of bleeding hearts like the Aztecs. Love was only a desperate struggle to find a happiness she didn't believe in, a happiness which, once realized, consumed people in its flames.

Contreras listened in such a state of confusion that his wounded pride was made unimportant by his bewilderment. For this woman was not saying that she didn't love him, but that she was refusing him precisely because she did love him. Her reasons were not those of virtue but of calculation.

It was the sixteenth century, active and full of illusions, against the twentieth, skeptical and rational. It was the dynamic force of heart and will against the static force of mental bookkeeping. It was Captain Contreras with all his world against the world of Paca Revilla.

And she won. Little by little Contreras' arguments dwindled. Paca's voice was kindly, sure and courageous. She got up. Contreras stayed where he was, staring numbly at the wall, his back to her. Paca went behind him and laid her hands on his shoulders tenderly, letting her fingers slip smoothly down his arms. Contreras did not move even when she leaned over him with their faces almost touching. Finally, without another word, she left.

When I got back that night I saw a light in Contreras' suite and went in. He was sitting on the sofa with his back to the door. He turned when he heard me. He told me not to wake him up in the morning because he was tired and wanted to sleep late. When I called him at noon the next day the bird had flown. The concierge said he had left at dawn with his luggage.

CHAPTER TEN

GOOD LORD, what a mess, what a bloody mess! No one can imagine what I went through trying to locate Contreras. How had he been able to leave? He hadn't the foggiest idea how to do anything for himself. How in the devil had he been able to get out of the country with all the interminable complications and red tape?

The first person I went to see was Paca at her hotel. Her reaction, of course, was one of surprise. Then she became angry at me. Why the hell should she know anything about the Captain, she wasn't his wet nurse or his manager.

"Out of here, you nosy, meddling — "

The next day, and the next, and the next she called me to plead for any news of the Captain.

I waited several hours to tell Dr. Yuste, putting it off. He had become increasingly vague lately and wasn't much help on anything. But finally I had to tell him because the Captain's disappearance had a certain emergency aspect: the charge account was in his name. On hearing my news the doctor actually began to cry. Why hadn't he waited another day? At least until after the banquet!

Up until now things couldn't have gone better. Professors from all over the country had been making intensive studies at the University. At the beginning the President had stood before the faculty and said, "If the experiments which we plan to make give as good a result as our preparations may presume, we shall be able to state the result officially."

After minutely studying and testing all the facets of Dr. Yuste's brilliant thesis, the University had arranged a session in which Contreras, subjected to hypnotism and a lie detector, had been analyzed and studied, not only by doctors of medicine but by historians, philologists, geographers, navigators and astronomers. Contreras' knowledge of astronomy was surprising, but it stopped exactly at the point where that science had begun to advance after his death. The same thing with regard to navigation. In geography there was not a corner of the Mediterranean, not an islet, sandbank, current, wind, or bay which he did not know. He spoke Italian correctly, and smatterings of French, Greek, Turkish, and Arabic in the archaic vernacular. But it was his Castilian which, paradoxically enough, made the professor testing him in that language vote against him. He said Contreras was not speaking "a Castilian of yesterday with today's language imposed on it, but today's language with incrustations of yesterday's syntax and vocabulary."

This was easily accounted for, I tried to explain at the

time. Since his appearance in the cemetery until the present he had read, studied and listened only to modern Spanish. How would it be possible for his speech not to have been influenced by the language he heard everywhere, in the street, at home, and in theaters? It's a well-known fact that people lose their native tongue more easily in a country with a similar idiom than when they live in one whose language has other roots. For example, a Spaniard in Russia would preserve his native tongue until the end, whereas this would not be true if he were to live in Portugal, Italy or Argentina.

The history experiment was sensational. Contreras did not know — and this was with a lie detector! — who was the Secretary of State of the United States that very day, but he knew who was Viceroy of Naples in 1608. He did not know the current President of France, but he knew who was Ambassador from Spain to France when Henry IV was assassinated. He had never heard of Napoleon, Nelson, Washington, or Bolívar, but he knew the titles of three of Lope de Vega's plays which had been lost. He even remembered the names of the actors who played the roles in them. A difficult bit of research subsequently proved that they existed.

"Gentlemen," the President proclaimed solemnly one memorable afternoon, "we would never have come to our present conclusion, without doubt one of the greatest discoveries in the history of medicine, since it proves the possibility of an almost unlimited prolongation of life, without the sacrifice and firmness of an extraordinary man. Gentlemen, this man whom we have before us has been deprived of the practice of his medical profession in Spain for having dared to believe in what we've been investigating. We proclaim it to be the truth! A round of applause, gentlemen, for Dr. Yuste!"

While listening to the long, emotional salvo of applause Yuste had to remove the spectacles from his shiny, porous nose, blow on them, and clean them nervously with his handkerchief.

The night the Captain fled there was to be a great banquet in honor of Dr. Yuste. The Spanish Ambassador cabled that afternoon to Madrid that either the doctor be reinstated in his profession and publicly exonerated, or Spain would run the risk of being voted against by the United States in the next meeting of the United Nations.

CHAPTER ELEVEN

WHEN Captain Contreras arrived back in Spain he felt he'd regained his liberty. He didn't give a damn for his indebtedness to Yuste and to me and for all we'd done for him. He considered his obligation to Roosevelt University fulfilled since he had undergone observation for the three months stipulated in the clause of the contract (the same one which said his body was to be delivered after death to the scientists "who wanted to amuse themselves by opening me up from top to bottom like a hog"). The only thing that bothered him was having exceeded his agreement by half a week. Just a few days, yet enough for him to have been hurt in his encounter with Paca Revilla. "That extra time cost me dearly. If I had only come back sooner I would have no regrets now."

He went to see a friend of his, Pepe Castejón, the Marqués del Darro, the broken-down aristocrat.

"Señor Marqués," Contreras said, "if Your Excellency be good enough, let me confess to you."

He then told him in detail about his flight from New York, his irritation with his protectors, the scene with Paca Revilla and his wish to escape again, to flee from everybody.

Pepe heard him out; and for Contreras, talking and talking, he was good therapy. Every evening at about eight o'clock Contreras and Castejón met and walked in the Retiro Park, under the solemn roof of the chestnut trees, from Alcala to Angel Caído, from the Rosaleda to the Estanque, and on to Calle de la Independencia where they separated till the following evening.

José "Pepe" Castejón was the sole survivor of one of those aristocratic families that ruin themselves a little bit more with each generation; it was left to him to put an end to the remains of the fortune. But he even did this in a lordly manner.

When he inherited his parents' modest fortune he invested it in a printing firm which reprinted editions of the classics. He brought in a man from Valencia who came from a long line of printers, a specialist in reproducing engravings, a real artist, and they turned out beautiful books.

"Don't call me Señor Marqués," Pepe would say to all his employees, "call me Don José."

A rather easygoing bohemian bachelor, he did not use his title when he had money; he only began to use it when he was ruined.

One day a group of his workmen came into his office threatening to strike if he did not dismiss the chief printer from Valencia because he didn't belong to their socialist union.

Castejón knew very well the risk he ran by not giving in to them. A strike in those days — it was July, 1936 — meant utter ruin. He apologized to the men, but how could he dismiss, without any cause, an honorable man who had to make his living? He could not take the bread out of the man's mouth. He called the printer into his office and said in front of the other employees, "Antonio, I invite you to dinner at Lardy's. I have a hundred pesetas left and I'd like to enjoy them with you."

"Don José," said one of the strikers threateningly, "have you thought what this will mean to you? Have you really thought it over, Don José?"

"Today," was his only reply, "you will call me Señor Marqués." He said goodbye, took the printer's arm, left the office and went to dinner.

The strike took place and became a part of the labor movement of the Civil War. His printing press was burned, his chief printer shot by the workmen, and the Marqués joined the Liberation troops. Later he lost an arm on the Teruel Front. Today he works as an editor on a small magazine with a salary of eight hundred pesetas. From time to time he publishes books of his own verse, not bad at all, in beautiful numbered editions; after trying in vain to sell them he gives them away to the relatives and friends who financed the edition.

On the day Contreras first met him he stared at Castejón fixedly. Castejón was very tall and thin, the expression in his eyes absent-minded and sad. His empty coat sleeve rested in a side pocket. Contreras exclaimed that he was sure he'd known Castejón some place, but he couldn't remember where.

"Oh, yes, in Sicily," the Captain said suddenly. "I knew you in Sicily . . . But it was many years ago."

"Afraid not," said Castejón. "You see, I've never been to Sicily, and all I know about it is through some letters of an ancestor."

"I could have sworn," said Contreras frowning. Then: "That ancestor of yours — "

"He was Viceroy of Sicily, under Philip IV, I believe."

"Philip III," corrected Contreras. "Wasn't he the Duke of Feria?"

When Castejón wonderingly said that he was, Contreras' eyes filled with tears, and he tried to kiss the Marqués' hand, swearing that there had never been a finer gentleman, more courageous, more generous, gentler with his subordinates, yet firm with the haughty than Don Lorenzo Suárez de Figueroa y Córdoba, second Duke of Feria. "He died of a quartain in 1607."

"What is a quartain, Papa?" Dorita Rivas asked her father who was with them.

"Fever," said Contreras, "today they call it fever."

During those months (when Yuste and I were traveling through the United States, Canada, Mexico and Uruguay giving lectures) Contreras had many new experiences. But he did not accept them with the same open-mindedness and enthusiasm as before. He visited a number of painting exhibitions, art museums and private collections, storing in his prodigious memory the date of each work of art which most offended his sensibility and, after a serious incident in the Prado Museum, he said to Castejón, "If you must be my confessor, sir, be so until the end. It seems I have blasphemed against art. I have sinned against it. But I do not repent."

Contreras became very agitated as he described his thoughts. There is nothing, he said, like the evolution of pictorial art for reflecting the true soul of the various epochs. When he died — or rather, when he fell into his long sleep — way back in his first life, Spanish art had attained to its maximum of glory, the highest peak of perfection.

"From purity of capriciousness, to restlessness, to mystic renunciation, to serenity, those are the steps corresponding to childhood, puberty, first and second youth, and maturity. Painting had its ages too. Fra Angelico: purity; Botticelli: capriciousness; El Greco: restlessness; Zurbarán: renunciation; Velázquez: serenity. Each one of them was faithful to his pictorial age. Then came upheaval but not chaos. After that I went to sleep. Now, upon awakening, I look at today's exhibitions. I stand before canvases spawned by the devil, masturbations of the conscience, excrement of Satan seen under a microscope, messy blobs and splotches, unformed masses, geometry by schizophrenics, colors which do not caress the eye but merely soil the canvas.

"Look, sir. A lack of perspective, gentleness and simplicity of form was fine in the authentic primitives, and they were products of their age. But these false primitives move one to laughter. It's as though a wrinkled old prostitute were to curl her hair and put a ribbon in it, then go out wearing socks and a short skirt, carrying a bunch of daisies to pose for a painter. Purity, sir, is not to be imitated. The days of the Battle of San Quintín, the days of *La vida es sueño*, the days of Alvarez de Menchaca and Fray Vitoria had for their illustrators Michelangelo and Velázquez. The days of gasoline and the atomic bomb, Nuremberg and Karl Marx had first Picasso then the Uglifiers."

He took from his pocket a colored reproduction of one of the most admired pictures in a current exhibit. Its lower part was like a mass of living matter: an unformed muscle, unattached to anything, and covered with slimy scales. Over this, like smudges or stains, like toboggans on a landslide of painting, were all the colors of the palette.

"Do you know the story of this painting?" After Castejón had replied in the negative Contreras went on: "The painter — it's an open secret that he's a pervert — was trying to illustrate the first poem in a book of verse by a famous poet as effeminate as himself. He worked night after night searching for the inspiration to give plastic form to those verses, a poem entitled Zero. He began to paint what you see here at the bottom of this reproduction. One night, he lost his temper and, after spitting on his work, he hurled his palette at it, hoping to smash it. Then he went to bed.

"Next morning he was awakened by the poet Redondo, who embraced him for having reproduced so exactly the celestial emotion of his verses. It seems that the wet paint on the palette had stuck to the wet paint on the canvas and during the night the palette had fallen to the floor by its own weight dragging blobs of paint down the canvas. 'Hug me, Basino, hug me!' the poet cried in ecstasy. 'What an agony of landslides, what an uprooting of brush strokes! What a tragic blending of colors on the lower levels of renunciation! I could never have dreamed of anything so appropriate· for my *Number Zero.* Your work fits into mine like a navel in the belly!"

"Would you change our times for yours?" asked the Marqués. "I understand that you didn't use to think like that."

"I don't know, I don't know," answered Alonso, and he put his hands to his head in a gesture of weariness.

Castejón gave a little laugh. "Don't take it all so seriously."

For the Marqués del Darro this was all just a topic for conversation, while for Contreras it was something quite vital.

"All right, all right," said Castejón lightly, "if you're looking for absolution I absolve you from your sins since they were only thoughts. If you don't actually cause scandal it isn't a serious sin."

Contreras burst out: "But you see, I have!"

"What do you mean? What have you done?"

Contreras then told Castejón about the affair now known to everybody as "The Scandal of the Goya Room." I was in Montevideo, South America, when the papers published the story. Count Foxá telephoned me from the Spanish Embassy to read me the cable sent by the United Press. When I heard it I shook. A few more scandals of this kind, I thought, and Contreras would land in jail. And Castejón must have thought the same thing when Alonso casually told him about it.

It seems that Contreras, obsessed by what he called
the prostitution of Art, decided to find out just where the
road began which forsook beauty and started the "search
for inspiration in the very bowels of ugliness." A group
of foreign students, invited by a major college, were visiting the Prado Museum. A famous lecturer had prepared
some pamphlets for them. There was polite applause following the brief presentation of the lecturer made by
the College President. The lecturer then took the pamphlets out of his pocket and announced that he would
speak about "The creator and high pontiff of modern
painting." At this moment a powerful voice thundered
and reverberated through the gallery, drowning out the
lecturer's words.

"Now I have you, spawn of Satan!" the voice said.
"Now I know who you are, villain!"

The voice, first heard in the Goya Room, became
louder as Captain Contreras approached.

When the Captain came suddenly upon the students,
among whom were Burmese, Egyptians, Filipinos, Dutch-
men, Cubans, Chileans, and a few Spaniards, he was not
in the least disconcerted. On the contrary, he leaped upon
the opportunity and gesticulating with his cane to em-
phasize his points, he delivered a blasting philippic
against the genius, the high pontiff, the emperor of modern painting.

"He is the one who has broken the molds of beauty
modeled by the Greeks! He is the first one to find the
finest theme of his inspiration in the Witches' Sabbath —
that demoniac rite where witches offer maidens to the
Devil in the form of a He-goat." He pointed to the *Naked*

Maja: "He is the first to use the aristocracy as a pornographic theme." He gestured away toward *The Family of Charles IV*: "He is the first to make a caricature out of the Sacred Catholic Monarchy! Raise monuments to him, dedicate dirges and threnodies to him, glorify him with hymns of praise, for he is the one who knocked beauty, gallantry and respect from their pedestals to set witches, toads and revolutions in their place!"

The foreign students, who had spent three boring days visiting museums, cities, monuments, streets, plazas and archives, who had been subjected to the tortures of three lectures and two recitations a day, and had looked on with unconcealed horror as the lecturer took out his pamphlets, found the interruption delightful. Even though most of them did not understand half of what Contreras was saying, they gave him an enthusiastic ovation when he paused.

The lecturer stammered one or two incoherent phrases and the College President hurried to notify the guards. When the guards ran into the lecture hall ready to restore order there was great confusion. For they saw a distinguished-looking gentleman addressing the students who were listening to him quietly and they saw that a presumptuous young man was trying to interrupt him, pulling at his jacket and exclaiming indignantly, so without further ado they grabbed the lecturer and carried him away by force, paying no attention to his protests.

Contreras, very much at ease now, took an Egyptian girl student by the hand (he afterwards said that she was a Goddess of Beauty) and led her, followed by all the others, first to the portraits of Sánchez Coello and the

Rubens and Titian Galleries, then to the Goya Room.

"Tell me, Beautiful Lady, and tell me, you friends of hers, which would you prefer — to see her painted by the gallant eloquence of those artists or sacrifice her modest beauty to the He-goat of this Goya who makes dirt of beauty?"

This comedy of errors, of course, couldn't last very long. In a short time the guards realized their mistake and, reinforced by the College President and the lecturer, began chasing Captain Contreras. Chuckling merrily the while, he led them a wild chase through the corridors. Once he let himself be cornered and then agilely ducked and feinted his way out, his cane on high, like a saber. Two of the students protected him by tripping some of the guards. At one point the Egyptian girl slapped the lecturer. Some of the spectators brayed indignantly that they never heard of such a disgraceful thing while others doubled over with laughter upon hearing Alonso's gleeful exclamations and seeing how skillfully he dodged the guards.

"Sir, with Your Majesty's pardon," said Contreras, in the Velázquez Room, bowing deeply in front of the portrait of Philip IV. Then he drew an imaginary line on the floor with his cane: "Whoever crosses this line I shall smash to the floor."

No one moved. Protecting his back, he edged along the wall till he was near the door. Then he leaped like a deer over the balustrade and out into the street. The last words he heard were those of the disconsolate Egyptian girl: "Comme il est beau et comme il est adorable."

CHAPTER TWELVE

ONE EVENING Castejón suggested to Contreras that they go to the house of some girls he knew and have a few drinks.

"Just do me a favor and don't tell them that you're the man found in Almudena because they'll think I'm joking and it'll be a bore."

"All right," he agreed. They began walking toward the house.

"They're working girls," Pepe explained, "and they split the rent for apartment and food. They don't earn much, and what they do earn they spend on clothes. They dress so well that if you ask them out to dinner no one can tell that they aren't from the best families."

"What do they live on?"

"One's a model at a famous dress designer's, another's a nurse, another one has a beau in the Administration who gets them groceries wholesale. They're all right, you'll see."

They arrived at the apartment building on the Avenida de la Reina Victoria. It was handsome and modern. The girls lived on the top floor. As it was summer the electricity was limited so they had to walk up the five flights of stairs. Contreras rang the bell, but Castejón rapped on the door since the electric bell did not work. An eye appeared in the peephole and behind it a female voice.

"Oh, it's the Marqués. You alone?"

"I've brought a friend."

"Wait a minute while I put on a dressing gown."

A few seconds later she opened the door.

"Excuse me for receiving you like this. I was in the bath when I heard you at the door." She turned to Castejón. "You've been forgetting me lately."

"This is my friend." He presented Contreras.

"Pepe's friends are automatically mine," she said with a nice smile.

A voice called from another room: "Loly, who's there?"

"It's the Marqués," Loly called back.

"Be there in a minute."

"Who's that?" Pepe asked.

"It's Sylvia, a new friend."

Loly took Contreras and Castejón by the arm and led them into the sitting room. It had a radio, a green sofa, two green armchairs, a green hassock and french doors that opened onto a terrace. The wood on the arms of the sofa and chairs was imitation mahogany. The walls and floor were very clean. On the terrace there was a green canvas lounge and a row of potted geraniums.

Loly was twenty-seven years old. She was slim, pretty, rather tall and charming. She laughed and chatted constantly. She wore a white dressing gown with large blue polka dots. When Sylvia came in Loly introduced everyone.

They brought out the drinks and turned on the radio. ("Not too loud — the neighbors are bores.") They danced, they drank, they laughed.

Sylvia was very slender and well made. She was not tall but so well proportioned that she seemed to be. She had very white skin and great sad eyes. She had an easy smile but rarely laughed. When she saw that Contreras did not care to dance particularly she took him out to the terrace and dropped down on the lounge. He sat at her feet and began to pay her compliments. She let him talk and she smiled now and then. Pepe and Loly had left the sitting room. Sylvia began to hum a song and then sang it softly.

> *You call me weathervane*
> *For being so fickle, fickle*
> *If I am a weathervane*
> *You're the wind, the wind,*
> *For the weathervane without the wind*
> *Doesn't move.*

"The weathervane without the wind stays quiet," said Alonso, thinking over the words. "Did you make it up?"

"Do I look like a poet? No, it's a popular song."

"Do you like poetry?"

"Very much."

"Listen to this one I wrote. It has to do with weather-vanes also."

I should like to be the wind, so I could catch you unawares,
To have the feel of my breath stir you—
Weathervane of my soul, my Filis,
So I might feel it is you without having you.

Sylvia leaned forward, genuinely interested.

"Did you write that?"

"Yes, I'm afraid it's not very good."

"Honestly did you write it?"

"By Jupiter, I swear it."

"I like the way you talk."

Almost all the nearby houses were dark. Those who were taking the air on other terraces were in the dark, enjoying the night needled with stars. The sky was high and far away.

"Recite it to me again."

He did so.

"Why that 'To feel that it is you, not having you'?"

"I don't know. Perhaps because, although I have lost hope of possessing, I still keep the hope of suffering."

"No one uses those words any more. We never speak of suffering in this house." Her lips smiled but her eyes were serious. "And — who is Filis?"

"I don't know."

"You mean, you don't want to say."

"I really don't know. Maybe a woman I knew in Palermo, a long time ago. She could be Isabel for whom I fought once. It could be Paca. It could be you."

"I?" Sylvia laughed. "No, my strange friend, I don't

care for that 'to feel that it is you, not having you' business!"

"Why not?"

"Because, well, because I don't." She smiled. Then:
"Has — has the Marqués told you anything about us?"

"For instance?"

"Oh, nothing."

Sylvia got up and leaned on the railing. Alonso stood
beside her looking at the street and the night.

When Loly and Castejón returned to the sitting room
it was late. They said goodbye and Sylvia added: "I'm
always home after nine-thirty. Oh, I forgot — what's
your name?"

"Alonso . . . Alonso Guillén."

"Maybe I'll be seeing you again, Alonso."

Twice a week Contreras played hooky from his walks
with Castejón. And generally when he did meet his
friend he'd leave shortly afterwards to go to the Avenida
de la Reina Victoria. He made no secret of it. The hours
passed easily with Sylvia on that terrace. Sometimes
Castejón would go with him and they'd visit the girls
together. But most of the time he went alone.

Contreras was tired. At times he felt an almost ir-
resistible desire to go away, he didn't know where, but
to go far and to go alone. He still had money left over
from the payment advanced for the use of his corpse, so
he could have left at any time, but somehow he didn't.
Sometimes he would get up in the morning determined
to take a train and wake up the next morning in a port
where he might sail to some place, any place: Messina,
Cairo or Astypalea.

But the days went by, and his energy with them, as he planned a trip that did not materialize. Contreras was going through a crisis of the spirit, a depression which, common to men of action, became with him who was action personified, a serious matter. People bored him, the theater enervated him, the cinema frightened him, music made him sad.

"The sick dialogue of a sick generation," he said one day commenting on a popular so-called comedy.

And as he said it he realized that he had changed or was changing his concept of men and the things around him. He thought long about this; was it restlessness or disillusionment?

Sometimes he would tell Sylvia about his restlessness.

"You're a philosopher," she'd say, "and a bit of a saint."

The first time he heard himself called a saint he burst out laughing. But later he began to grow fond of the idea and even began thinking of ending his days in a hermitage. "It's just that I am growing old," he said morosely. "Others, when they're aging, begin to get hoarse and to cough, but I am beginning to think."

"To think?" repeated Sylvia. "Is that so bad?"

"Who knows?"

If we wished to reduce to narrow terms each one of the complex states of mind experienced by Contreras from his disinterment until the end, we would have to group them into three parts: dazzled euphoria, the reformer-critic, and — discouragement. If the last was the most pathetic and the first the most ingenuous, the one he was experiencing now was perhaps the most brilliant. He defended himself against the shadows which pressed on him, overwhelming him. Only Sylvia heard him without argument. When other people shut him up with arguments he was unable to answer, he took refuge with her. One day, in a rage, he told her how he'd been insulted.

"What happens," a young avant-guardist had said in an impudent, challenging tone, "is that you old malcontents can't stand the fact that there's a political regime in Spain that's been in power for so many years."

"Whippersnapper!" roared Contreras. "If I have any objection to the regime it is not that it's lasted for a dozen or so years but that it will not last for two hundred. If it would I'd subscribe to it this minute!"

"You should stay away from arguments like that," Sylvia ventured to say.

The Captain's mental attitude toward our world was at a similar stage to that of the sixteenth century Aztecs when they discovered that the horses and riders of the Conquistadors were not one gigantic body but two distinct beings: two beings who could die even as themselves of a lance-thrust in the heart, two beings, furthermore, who were imperfect and against whom they could fight, whom they might conquer . . .

In the midst of all the tremendous advances of modern society Captain Contreras discovered meanness, lies, and values so misplaced that the achievements he'd so admired were steadily being obliterated. Once upon a time Contreras had glorified technique, man's great talent; but now he began to suspect that man was a prisoner of technique, reduced to being the instrument, not the master of his own works. He saw it everywhere. Man, creator of the machine, found himself submitting to it, a slave to it. The very people who created the State had to submit to the State in order to achieve its ends. The State was no longer at the service of the Nation; it was the Nation which was at the service of the State, and the elephantiasis of the State, already begun in the earlier days of Contreras, had spread itself beyond limits, whether in monarchies or republics.

But what astonished him most was the confusion around the concept of sovereignty. Where does sovereignty reside, in the Prince who commands or in the people who obey? He didn't understand these philosophies. Power, the theologians said, emanated from God, and the King exercises it in His name. But now some French executioners (Contreras spoke of "now" to include the French Revolution) had imposed the idea that sovereignty resided in the people, and the whole universe supported this idea. Whoever commanded no longer did so in the name of God but in the name of the people.

If the people had really become of age, as the Liberals said (Paca Revilla's father more heatedly than anyone), then it was right that they should govern themselves, electing officials from among themselves.

"But tell me, dear sir," Contreras exclaimed when he heard this, "who are these people of whom you speak and in whom rests the sovereignty? Are these part of them — the gypsies, the Moors, the ignorant, the poverty-stricken, thieves, prostitutes, and those castoffs living in caves or in the mountains who have never been exposed to even the most primitive civilization or education? What have Goya's witches and their Sabbath to do with affairs of government? They are entitled to human rights, of course, but you don't endow them with political responsibility, for they simply don't have it. If you want to give them some representation all right, but don't allow them an equal vote with honest and educated men.

"Redact your Constitution, sir, maintain it, and when you have done so call me and I'll be glad to be a deputy."

Contreras always spoke as though he had a lot of people hanging on his words, even when he had an audience of one unattentive and unitelligent one. But when he saw that his ideas weren't getting through at all, he'd give up with a sigh and retreat. Then he'd run to Sylvia. And Sylvia, whose best virtue was to listen, or at least pretend to listen, began to entwine herself slowly, sweetly, into his soul.

One night, Contreras was drinking. Sylvia encouraged him by drinking too, because she wanted to see him a bit gay. Instead, the more he drank the more he withdrew into himself.

"How tiresome you are sometimes! Why don't you talk?"

"Excuse me. I was dreaming awake."

"Not very gallant of you!"

Sylvia, half bored and half mellow, sat on his knees, kissed him, stifled a yawn, and curled up comfortably.

"It is late. It will soon be dawn."

"Don't go! It's so nice like this."

"But if I stay I'll start to talk. Today I have voices within me that want to come out . . . and I don't know whether you wish to hear them . . ."

"Talk, talk. I love hearing your voice so near me. Sometimes it makes me feel all warm and I like it."

"Look! Did you see? A shooting star!"

"How can I — I have my eyes closed to hear you better."

"Sylvia!"

It was important.

"Yes?"

"I want to buy a house and land near here."

"Near here? Where?"

Contreras began to talk. He spoke in low tones, intimately, and with emotion. He had the feeling that he had spoken the same words long ago in another life; perhaps in Sicily when he had thought of leaving the Army; perhaps when the first threads of silver appeared over his temples and the King's secretaries refused to reward his services; perhaps when, in his plumed hat and finery, he had heard the Countess of Monterrey's mirthful laugh.

"A quarter of a league from Toledo," he began and his speech seemed to become more ancient as he talked, "there where the Tagus leaves the Cantabrian Sea to face Portugal, I should like to buy an orchard. The house will be already built but the land must be cultivated and cleared of stones for planting. A big house, but not big enough to make the neighbors envious, nor so small that

I shall have to envy them. I shall retire to rest, for I must."

He paused.

"Go on, go on," whispered Sylvia.

"The ground floor will have a hearth for the fire, and two chairs near it, one as high as the tall-backed chair of a studious monk, and a smaller one to attend the hours. Against the wall there will be a simple oak table; the top will be hewn from one piece of wood and the feet will be fashioned like lion's claws to make a steady base. On the table there will be an inkstand with a goose-quill pen and sand to dry the ink. The inkstand will be of bronze carved with the figure of St. John on the Island of Patmos writing the Apocalypse. At the right of the table there will be a few good books, both sacred and profane. Among the first there will be à Kempis, among the second *The King without a Kingdom,* by Lope. Over the table will hang the Arms of the King. Against the front wall there will be an astrolabe, a compass, spurs, and an arquebus, not to defend the house but to show that who lives there knows how to use the weapons of both land and sea. The wall will be whitewashed without any decorations but an image of Our Lady of Grace in glazed tile, for they do this very well in Talavera.

"Next to the image there will be a lighted oil lamp, and next to the table a greyhound who will serve for hunting as well as for guarding the house. On a shelf near the books we will keep a chessboard, because that game is not for lazy people but for soldiers. The chessmen will be of ivory, one side Turks, the other, Christians. At the other end of the room there will be an embroidery frame, a spinning wheel and a lute. You will embroider or spin and I shall play music for you, for a soldier who has lived at the courts of princes can do anything. At dawn I shall go hunting, in the afternoon I shall attend to my estate, and if the nights are long I shall sing you some songs which gave me a bit of fame even if my services to the King did not. For an old soldier has to change his own life, rather than have his vanities and weaknesses change it for him.

"It is better to retreat in time than to make a forced march, and better to be ashamed once than to be one hundred times jaundiced. I have always wanted to retire and lead the life of a nobleman for, though my ancestors were not noble, there is no reason why my grandchildren should not be so.

"On Fridays we shall feed ten beggars. I shall wash their feet and you will serve them at the table, for one must prepare the soul for the crisis that is so long in coming, and what one has not done in many years one may do in a short time if the goodwill is there. On Sundays we shall visit the neighbors unless they have announced a visit to us. We can arrange that in the morning after High Mass in the Cathedral.

"We shall not be famous for our deeds but for our virtues, for what one has not gained in youth one may gain in old age. I shall be skillful in the hunt and you in honesty. You will be prudent with your maids, severe if they are wanton but gentle with their weaknesses, for good council does more good than bad punishment, and a good example preaches better than words.

"I am old for war but not for love, for one knows this

without testing it, by the way women look at one, not by the way one looks at women; eagerness for love may deceive him who aspires to it, but not him who is aspired to."

There was a long silence. Sylvia did not answer. Sylvia, sitting on his knees with her head on his breast, had fallen asleep. She had been sleeping almost since his first words.

In the distance the blackness of the night seemed to be changing its hue, as though a herald of the dawn had rubbed the horizon with turpentine. And Sylvia was asleep.

"Sylvia, Sylvia, do you wish to unite with me in holy matrimony?"

The reply was silence.

Contreras, raising his voice and tightening his arm around her waist, went on: "I have strength left, and money, and I do not lack the gratitude that would thank you for accepting."

At his gesture and voice Sylvia awoke with a little start.

"Does my proposal surprise you? Sylvia, for the last time, do you want to marry me?"

"*I* marry? You want to marry *me?*

She passed a hand over her face as though to bring herself to her senses. Then she pressed even more closely against him.

"Marry . . . marry . . . But you don't know who I am!"

Contreras answered with a question:

"Do you, by chance, know who *I* am?"

CHAPTER THIRTEEN

Who was this girl whom Contreras wanted?

Who was Sylvia?

No doubt the reader will have guessed her secret, even as I did as soon as I found out about her sentimental relationship with my fugitive friend. When I returned from South America I began to investigate her background to save Contreras from the stupid net he wanted to fall into, for personal reasons, and to satisfy my literary curiosity. I soon discovered the importance the new character would have for this book, not only because of the influence she would have on the Captain's life, but because Sylvia was a product of our society, this society which I'm so immersed in that I'd never have come to understand it if Contreras hadn't revealed it to me indirectly. A good painting needs shadows if it is to be complete. And Sylvia was a shadow, a shadow of our society.

Who was Sylvia?

The Sylvia of today was called Concepción yesterday. She was the daughter of a bank clerk in Villanueva del Río. He was such a punctilious, honest clerk that he resembled the father in Benavente's *Pepa Doncel,* whose daughter said that he'd been so honorable all his life that when he died he left his daughters in the difficult position of not being able to be honorable. When her father died Sylvia left Villanueva and came to Madrid with twenty summers behind her, half a dozen dresses, a few thousand pesetas, and many ambitions. She had the clothes and pretensions of a provincial young lady. She didn't want to be a salesgirl because she was a lady, and a young lady cannot live on a sixty-duro salary. She did not wish to work in an office because, not knowing shorthand, the salary would have been less than the salesgirl's; nor a kindergarten teacher, because she would have earned less than in an office; nor, of course, a governess, for her parents had never been in service, and this was hardly her goal. She came to Madrid to be married. In the meantime she would find something in some important position with someone important. "Something, somewhere, someone," Sylvia would repeat without losing hope.

Finally she found a job. Mentally, that is. She wanted to be an airline hostess. She knew French, she knew geography. She went to the offices of an airline. But the French of the Villanueva nuns was not exactly the French spoken in France. Besides, she would have to learn English. How long would it take her to learn and perfect a language which, until then, she thought she knew?

First she thought, in three months. Then six. Later on, in a year. And she began that dreadful race between the difficult apprenticeship and her funds — which she kept locked in a box. If she got the job before her funds ran out . . . But if the money ran out before she got the job? Sylvia began to study, first in her hotel, afterwards in a small room in a boardinghouse.

When she met Fernando her worries became less pressing, for he asked her to apéritifs which she ate to supplement her lunch, and he invited her to dinner so that she could stretch out her funds a day or two more.

The story is so commonplace and vulgar that it is scarcely worth writing for publication. On the other hand, I feel the urge to preach and moralize, which is hardly my forte. But I can't curb the displeasure which Sylvia's story makes me feel. It isn't vulgar in the English sense of the word — low and gross — but in the sense of frequent, widespread, the daily fare of our society. Before — it's hard to pin down just how long ago "before" was — the commerce of flesh was nourished by the lowest depths of society; the public conscience refused to cry *mea culpa* because they were beyond all civic redemption — or, at least, *easy* redemption. Schools and the Church couldn't reach them. They were poor country people who emigrated to the big city, hypnotized by its false lights. I don't say they weren't worthy for society to intone a *mea culpa* over, I'm just saying that society didn't do it. It was like a wound so difficult to heal that discouraged doctors abandoned the case, declaring it to be incurable.

But never has the level from which prostitution is supplied risen so high as today. It now approaches the middle-class; it has penetrated openly into what other countries, like France, call the bourgeoisie. And so it has reached the level of everyone's responsibility; it's in our own field, within reach of doctors and medicine, that is if there are doctors and medicine that can cure it.

The steps to Sylvia's downfall were not many. The first was her own upbringing: she had not been trained for work. (That was for men or for servants: Sylvia was *a young lady*.) The second was when her father turned away a suitor.

"That little nobody? Don't even speak of it! He's not for you!"

The third was her father's death, and her coming to Madrid. Later on, the meeting with Fernando. The penultimate step. Let us stop a minute on the penultimate step.

For several hours the sun had been pouring into the bedroom window. Sylvia half opened her eyes and looked at her watch. It was three o'clock in the afternoon. She got up, went blindly to the washbasin and poured a glass of water. She took two aspirins, swallowed a little water, closed the curtains to dim the glare, and went back to bed. Her head was bursting. She'd drunk too much the night before, and her eyes and her temples hurt. She'd never drink again, at least not so much. Yesterday had been fun. How amusing Andrés was, that doctor friend of Fernando's! From the time they left Madrid in the car until they arrived at the restaurant in La Coruña, she had done nothing but laugh at his wit and his stories. His girl was very nice too. But they drank too much. *"We drank too much,"* Sylvia corrected herself. "It was crazy." Fernando has become too affectionate and caressing. Sylvia did not like this public love-making. "Fernando! They're looking at us!" "But, my dear, just look at *them!*" Sylvia vaguely remembered the scene on the sofa between Andrés and his girl. "Why don't they wait till they're alone? It's disgusting!"

Sylvia's head throbbed so much that it hurt her to think. Nevertheless she wanted to remember everything.

Fernando took a taxi to Madrid while Andrés stayed there with the car. The taxi had to stop twice before she got home because . . . because she was so . . . so drunk that she got sick and vomited all over the car. "How repulsive, my God! What Fernando must think of me!"

Remembering this, Sylvia covered her face with her hands, mortified. She couldn't remember any more. It was too shameful to remember more. She got up to get dressed, but everything started to spin around so she went back to bed. She stayed there dozing, but could not fall asleep. Fernando had left her at the *pensión* . . . and come with her to her room. He had gone away and come back.

"Look, sorry, but I don't have any money for the taxi."

"There in the box . . . take it. You can return it tomorrow."

"You only have a thousand pesetas? Shall I take it?"

"Take it. You can bring it back tomorrow."

"I'll go pay the taxi, then I'll bring you the change."

Sylvia remembered no more. She couldn't remember whether Fernando had come back or not. She dozed on. My God! Drunk and on the bed without undressing! She had slept in her clothes all night. How would her dress look? She tried to feel her dress, but — she was naked. Then she remembered Fernando's form, excited, rough and brutal. What had happened? No, she didn't want to remember it. She jumped out of bed and went to the money box. It was empty. Sylvia found herself staring at her image in the mirror, most of her lipstick eaten away, great circles under her eyes and her hair in tangles. Sylvia gazed, and in spite of everything she had the sensation in a flash of seeing that she was beautiful. She spat at her face in the mirror, enjoying the sight of her suffering reflection. She wanted to react and could not. And the money box lay open in front of her, empty.

Eleven months later Sylvia's money box was full again. Not in the *pensión* either, but in an apartment taken for her with other girls in the Avenida de la Reina Victoria. There she could receive her friends, and they carried on, as well as they could, a sad comedy. But a legitimate comedy.

All these girls had two groups of men; one group knew their profession, and from this group they accepted money and gifts, but never received them in the apartment. The other group did not know what their profession was, and were kept in ignorance for there was always the bare hope of marriage and a change of luck. In the afternoon, from four to nine, Sylvia went to Doña Trini's house to sell the pleasures of her body. At night, before going to bed, she shut herself in her room to study commercial English and to rectify the French taught by the nuns in Villaneuva, or she read poetry, or she wrote her mother, excusing herself for not going to see her, but sending her money so that her little brother could go on with his studies and make something of himself. She hadn't seen Fernando again, not even to ask him for the money, which, of course he hadn't repaid.

It was only years afterwards, when I came to know her well, that Sylvia told me about the afternoon following the incident begun on the road to La Coruña. When she was finally calm enough to reason with herself she decided to go home to her mother and find "something" there with "somebody . . ." who might help her. But the vagueness of these words compared to the reality of having to eat the next day, and the next, stopped her. Since the box was empty she had to choose between spending what she had in her purse on a train ticket home or on dinner that night. For of course the ticket could not be third class. She could not travel with peasants. After all, she was a young lady.

CHAPTER FOURTEEN

MY VISITOR didn't even give me a chance to decide whether it was convenient or not for me to see him that morning. The maid's announcement, "Sir, Mr. Morales is asking for you," was immediately followed by the entrance of the Police Commissioner.

"My dear Cornejo, how glad I am to see you again in our part of the world!"

"Morales! How nice to see you! Come in."

Morales gripped my hand with a cordiality and effusiveness that made me shiver, for it's a well-known fact that the amiability of policemen is in direct proportion to the gravity and delicacy of the affair in hand. A visit from a policeman? Bad. Cordiality in his manner? Worse.

"Well, how nicely you're fixed here, Cornejo! I hadn't thought of you as a man of such good taste."

"I don't know if I like your compliment or not," I replied, "because it was a decorator, not I, who fixed this all up."

"I'm glad. I'm glad your business is going well."

"Not bad, knock on wood."

"And — just what *is* your business, my friend, if you don't mind my asking?"

"My business, Señor Morales, is like the little squiggle that certain companies add after their names. It means 'engaged in an activity which benefits society.' I, too, use the little squiggle."

"Assuming that the activity is legal, naturally."

"Naturally."

Morales was rather a small man with large features, a huge mouth, small gray eyes and big flyaway ears. He frequently touched the back of his neck with his hands, giving it three quick congratulatory pats as though he were patting the haunch of a horse after a nice ride.

"When did you come back from South America?"

"Yesterday afternoon. I haven't unpacked yet."

"Come alone?"

"Look, Morales, you're a busy man and so am I, so let's try to save some time. The best way's for you not to ask questions which you already know the answers to. You know I came back yesterday. You know I came alone. And you know why I came. Ask me something you don't know and I'll gladly try to help you. I suspect that what you want is the same thing I want, namely, how to find Contreras, right?"

"I won't say that it isn't. But why do you want to find him?"

"Because, well, I won't say that my life depends on it, but my money, my business and my profession do. I'm not going to hide anything from you — no reason to. Sure I live off Contreras. I manage him. I am, how shall I say it — sort of his impresario. But in exchange for my frankness to you I'm going to ask you something: what business is all this of the police?"

Morales patted his neck, turned round in his chair, without saying anything, and his face opened into a lopsided smile.

I got up and pressed the bell.

"María, bring us some drinks. Which do you prefer, whiskey or sherry?"

"Sherry."

"Bring some sherry, María. But bring it into the office. We'll be better there."

Morales followed me; we crossed the sitting room and went into my study. This was more private, and besides, I had papers there which might be of interest to the Commissioner.

"Don't tell me, Morales, that you still doubt the authenticity of the Contreras case?"

"Oh, come now, it would be rather strange if I did believe it, don't you think?"

"Even after what happened in America?"

"Ah yes, I did hear something about a statement by some small college president, but I'd rather you told me about it."

María came in with the tray, left it on the table and went out. I poured the drinks. Morales sat in front of me. I began as eloquently as I could to give him a point by point description of the investigation as it had gone along. The scene of the lie detector; the study made by the philologists; the historians; the questions of the psychiatrist; the discussions; the lectures of Dr. Yuste and his election to the College of Medicine in America; and the uproar in the more sensational newspapers which didn't dare contradict the veracity of the case after Contreras had officially been declared a living miracle by the doctors of the university which owned his body.

I then took several documents bearing on the case out of the safe. "I am not giving you these to take, but if you want photostats to study at your leisure I'll have them made for you."

Morales began to look them over with undisguised curiosity. From time to time he would pause over one of them with a nasty little laugh and look up as though to say, "Don't think you're going to pull any fast ones on me . . . I'm too clever."

And Morales *was* clever. You can convince an intelligent man with reasons. But with clever ones — since they are impervious to reason — there's nothing to be done. The Spanish postwar in its first period brought to the surface — as rain does worms — various promotions of *clever* men. Suspiciousness, trickery, audacity, malice — all conditions born of an inferiority complex — are sometimes substitutes for their own intelligence but never for that of others, for the latter haven't the offensive weapons needed to pierce the armor of suspicion with which the *clever* ones protect themselves.

"Very interesting," said Morales, "extraordinarily interesting."

"Are you convinced?"

"Come, now, Cornejo, I can't really swallow all that New York stuff."

"Good Lord, what more proof do you want?"

Morales gave me some protective little pats on the back and said goodbye. When the door was half closed he suddenly opened it again.

"Say," he asked casually, "do you know where Contreras lives?"

"Not yet, but I'll find out."

"Save yourself the trouble. He's in an orchard near Toledo, the second kilometer on the Extremadura road. He's named the place Venezuela or Marizuela or something like that."

"It must be Valenzuela," I replied.

"That's it, but how'd you guess?"

"Oh, he had a friend by that name many years ago in Toledo."

"Well, Cornejo, got to get moving, goodbye."

"Wait a minute, Morales — tell me, what's he doing there? Who's he with?"

"Ask Castejón. He knows about it . . . and so do I."

And Morales, the *clever* man, left.

CHAPTER FIFTEEN

THE ROAD between Madrid and Toledo seemed about to melt under the sun, a sun that was a foundry oven. The mule-drawn carts left tracks on the asphalt like skis on snow. I was uncomfortable in the heat and uneasy about the risk of a blowout; uneasy, too, about the outcome of the business which was taking me to Toledo.

The immediate plan was to rescue Contreras from Sylvia's net. I *had* to. Dr. Yuste and I had started this business of bringing back a phantom to the world of reality and by God we were going to finish it.

In the past few years, both inside Spain and out, lots has been said and written about Contreras' miraculous longevity and of course many people, then and now, have said it was pure bunk. But whether they believe it or not, almost nobody credited Yuste and me for having made it all possible; without us Contreras would have been finished by the doubting Thomases early in the game. No one knows what scorn and ridicule we suffered and the cruelty of those people who, even after the evidence was accepted, still attacked us as though we were trying to pull something crooked . . . The Morales type — the clever men — never forgave our sacrifice. These lines are not being written to convince them, nor to deceive them. If anyone at any time wants to do research on the Contreras case they'll have to ultimately come to this book, for I'm withholding absolutely nothing — even to the oh-so-shocking fact that I hoped to get a little legitimate monetary return for all my efforts on the Captain's behalf.

If this book were less than the complete truth I suppose I'd try to give the impression that sheer affection for the Captain and altruism caused my distress over his having flown the coop. But why should I hide the fact that I was desperately afraid that with the bird flown, my usefulness was at an end? Once Yuste had been vindicated, the Captain's income assured, and his fame spread throughout the country, it was necessary to bring him out of confinement, and confront him with the great world. We had to expose him to the problems of today so that we might study patterns of conduct and thought from his reactions. But now, from our lenient supervised liberty, the bird had flown from his roomy cage to a much more confining one: behind the bars raised by a woman.

Morales told me where to find Contreras, Castejón gave me the news of Sylvia, and Conrado Blanco, manager of the Lara Theater, gave me the urgent and highly attractive motive for rescuing him; namely, five lectures

at two hundred pesetas a seat, two by Dr. Yuste with
Contreras present, and three by Contreras himself.
Twenty per cent of the gross would go to a corporation
consisting of Contreras, Yuste and myself. For my part
in convincing my friend, for the editing and correcting
of the lectures, and for publicity I would receive an extra
fee. The lectures would be repeated in Paris, London
and Rome, and finally in the provinces. But first I had to
get Contreras out of the clutches of that tramp of a
woman, no matter how.

Near Toledo I turned off on the Extremadura road.
All the way I had been reviewing in my mind what the
girls in the Avenida de la Reina Victoria had told me
about this Sylvia whom I was about to get rid of . . .

Upon reaching the second kilometer a freshly painted
sign on a stake pointed to a detour. I read: *Half a league,
Valenzuela Orchard.* I turned into an oxcart road and
had to close the windows because of the dust. Then the
road, or whatever it was, suddenly vanished into a plowed
field. I got out. There was no sign of any kind here, nor
a living soul to be seen, nor a house of any sort. Abrupt
hills, and here and there an oak, a chestnut, or a walnut
tree. In the distance "black poplars, poplars of the
shore," the poplars of Antonio Machado. I know the country from literature only (which I sincerely believe is the
only way to bear it), so I wouldn't swear that those were
the trees described by Machado.

Everything was wrapped in a silence. There was great
peace. Words which always have bothered me: silence
and peace. Both of them make me uneasy. They bore

me. But I was reassured by the thought — as I climbed a little hill which seemed like a mountain to me — that all this must bore Sylvia, too. Maybe it'd be a good idea to try to convince her how boring it was. But I rejected the idea, at least for the moment. What I'd have to do with Sylvia was improvise, play it strictly by ear and intuition as I went along.

From the top of the hill I saw the house. It was all white, half hidden among the chestnut trees that shaded it. When I came nearer I saw that it was very large. I went to the front door. The silence there was as great as in the surrounding countryside. Either no one lived there or they were asleep. I called out twice and was about to shout again when a boy came running from the garden and motioned me to be quiet. He stepped in front of me and said nothing, waiting for me to speak. Brilliant dialogue followed:

"Anyone home?"

"Yes."

"Who?"

"Me."

"Anyone else?"

"Yes."

"Who?"

"The master."

"Why didn't you say so?"

"Because you didn't ask me."

"Well. I want to see him."

"You can't now."

"Why not?"

"Because you can't."

"A lady here by the name of Sylvia?"

"No."

"No?"

"No!"

"Well what *is* the mistress' name?"

"Concepción."

"I guess I was misinformed, then."

"Yes, sir."

One had to get out this boy's answers with a corkscrew.

"Run and tell your master that his friend Cornejo is here. He'll come right away, you'll see."

"My master told me that if a man named Cornejo came I was not to let him in. He says that every day."

This took me back a bit.

"And if I give you twenty duros will you tell your master I'm here?"

"No."

"Why not?"

"Because the master says he hangs traitors from trees."

"I don't seem to be doing too well."

"Yes, sir. I mean no sir."

"Listen, do you like your master?"

"Yes, sir."

"Why?"

"Because he is my master."

"Oh, God."

At this point the voice of Contreras shouted from inside: "Luigi, let that damned scribbler in!"

"Come in, sir."

I have accurately described my conversation with this boy, for I wrote the notes for this chapter that night. The name of Luigi with which Contreras had baptized him alarmed me, but this was only the beginning.

"What madness is this?" were the first words I was able to utter.

And madness was the only word for it. The house, the door, Luigi's clothes, even his name, hadn't been clues enough to warn me of the comedy that was being played inside those walls; because the furniture, the décor, and Contreras' clothes were all strictly seventeenth century.

The Captain had even let his beard grow. When he saw my astonishment he burst into laughter. I wanted to cry with dismay and anger. Two years' work demolished!

"Evidently you can't be left alone, Captain. Would you mind telling me what sort of craziness this is?"

"Calm down, Mr. Scribbler, and sit beside me because we must have a talk."

"We certainly must. May I ask you why you gave instructions not to let me in? It is obvious you don't want to see me, but what's less clear is why a person like me who's sacrificed himself so that you might live deserves to be treated like this. I've dropped everything in this world to serve you and to help you and I don't deserve this treatment, Contreras, I really don't. But aside from deserving it or not, there're a lot of things I want explained to me. What are you doing here in the first place? Whose house is this? Who are you hiding from? Why are you running away just when you could be on top of the world, when you could be the biggest thing in Spain?"

He listened to me, smiling sadly. He waited without becoming impatient — rare for him. When I had finished he pulled me down beside him, put his arm around my shoulder, and, looking me in the eye, said, "I am tired."

Then he lowered his eyes, as though ashamed of what he was going to say. He began to speak, hesitantly at first, then gaining assurance, as I'd never heard him speak before. His speech revolved around three obsessive themes: God, the universe, and salvation. If he had run away it was because he was beginning to lose his faith, not in God, but in the universe and his own salvation. Contreras had lost hope.

At first, he explained in his flowery way, everything seemed better than in his first life because all the advances of material order, technique and even politics, he considered to be a tremendous jump forward, "as though man were approaching his goal which was none other than perfection reflected in God."

But now he was beginning to think that the tremendous strides of humanity were not toward God but toward nothingness. God no longer mattered in man's plans and everything man had created had become an end in itself. If this was so, man's ultimate end had shrunk. Social good, the political system, the machine were not — as he had thought formerly — way stations overcome by man on his journey toward God's perfection, but goals in themselves on a road which led to nowhere.

I did not know, nobody living in our time could realize, how God used to be behind all man's endeavor, in

Contreras' golden time. The King represented the power inherited from God. The wars Contreras had taken part in were religious wars against the infidel in the Mediterranean, against the heretics in Europe, against the pagans in America. The sins of pride or anger or lust were flights from the royal road between God and man, but they were flight balanced by repentance which moved man to find the lost road and return to Him.

God was no longer behind man's endeavor. He was out of the program, He didn't even rate a gallery ticket to the great farce which was being played. This thought so dismayed Contreras that he had begun to think; he was obsessed by the futility of generation upon generation that had lived and died struggling for a better world. He thought of the Catholic Monarchy, of the Christian armies, of the heights attained by the creative work of poets, theologians, jurists, moralists and saints who had labored and led the world to — failure. He thought with despair of yesterday's hopes. Finally "Yuste's pride, Cornejo's superficiality, Paca Revilla's skepticism, Pepe Castejón's weakness and indecision, are the symbols of a Spain that is proud, skeptical, frivolous, inept and incapable, a Spain that lives on the smug assumption that it is the last refuge — what a grotesque paradox! — for the world's spirituality."

However, there was still a gap between this and complete skepticism, he asserted, and that was why he wanted to keep on the edge of the abyss, but on the side, on the shore, belonging to God. This shore was his "island of peace": his orchard, and the ropes that held his boat were the purity and the serenity of that holy woman who was with him.

I gave a start.

"Sylvia?" I asked.

"Her name is Concepción," he amended.

"That woman is exactly what I want to talk about."

Contreras looked at me with both interest and annoyance.

"You know her?"

"No, but I . . ."

"Then it is I and not you who will talk about her."

Contreras got up and, motioning to me to follow him, went outside. The sun's last rays had left a sepia stain on the horizon, and a gentle breeze consoled the earth which had been martyred all day by the heat. A few steps from the house, under the shade of the ancient chestnuts, Contreras stopped and offered me a wicker chair drawn up to a stone table. We sat down, and a servant brought a *bota* of wine.

"Every afternoon at this time," he said, "I sit here to watch the night fall, wetting my gullet with this rather nice wine from time to time."

He threw his head back, raised the leather wine bottle, and expertly squeezed a stream of red wine into his mouth.

The sky changed from red to lilac and from lilac to gray. Night was already calling at the door, and the crickets began a harsh musical reception for her.

Contreras passed me the *bota* and I drank.

Then he told me how during the last Carnival season

he'd had the amusing idea of acting out a pageant in period costumes. Castejón helped him, and the entire production was under the expert direction of the Teatro Español's director. The only people invited were actors, artists, poets, reporters and a few diplomats, all dressed in the period.

Contreras opened the parade on a splendid horse. He was accompanied by two trumpeters and four lackeys dressed in red silk ornamented with baldrics, golden swords and plumed hats. The pageant represented the arrival of the Cardinals, Sandoval, Espínola, and Albornoz at the palace of the Count of Monterrey in Rome where the Count was then, in 1630, Ambassador to His Majesty.

"What a costume I wore on that occasion!" Contreras seemed to be reliving it. "I carried a blue standard with silver flames, antelope shoes studded with gold embroidery, with sleeves and doublet the same, and a crest of blue, green and white plumes on my helmet."

He described how the procession had come down the esplanade to the house which represented the Monterrey palace, the arrival of the Cardinals in their carriage followed by all their suite. Contreras was waiting for them, and knelt on the ground for their blessing, then took them inside.

Near dawn, when the guests had left, Sylvia — I mean Concepción — who had played the part of the Countess rather shyly, was left alone with Contreras. She got out of the uncomfortable brocaded costume and went to him. The servants put out the torches and oil lamps which had illuminated the pageant and turned on the electric lights. Contreras, absolutely exhausted, watched them sadly from his high monk's chair. All that fantastic world which he had relived briefly was going up in smoke as daylight came. The servants opened the windows, and the pleasant odor of civet, amber and cured antelope, smelling like the back of a glover's shop, vanished. In the middle of that stage which was changing so quickly Captain Alonso de Contreras — with antelope shoes embroidered with gold, with sleeves and doublet the same — came painfully back to reality.

Concepción came to him and passed a hand over his forehead. "You're tired," she said. "You're sad."

He looked at her without speaking.

"It was so good to see you a little while ago. You were so happy, so full of life, you looked so young."

"You think I am old!"

"I think you are adorable!"

"Concepción!"

"Yes."

"You know the story they tell about me? That I am not a man of today but a survivor of another time, and that my grave is separated from my cradle by three centuries?"

"Yes, I know the story, but you've never spoken to me about it."

"Well — do you believe it? Do you believe that everything Yuste and Cornejo say about me is true?"

Sylvia seemed disconcerted and did not answer right away.

"You haven't said whether I ought to or not . . . but

I'd like to think about it a bit. Do you understand? It would frighten me . . ."

"It frightens me not to think of it. I am beginning to be afraid of roaming the world with my eyes blinded by the light of outside without ever looking inside of myself. Today, seeing myself dressed like this in front of those people who seemed like my friends from another life, I began to think that none of this had happened, and I was happy. But now that I am awake I feel disgust smothering me. I would like to wear these shoes and doublet always. I would like to wear this habit when I meditate, and I would like to have you always near to lean on when I weaken."

Contreras got up from his monk's chair, closed the windows, turned off the electric lights, lit the lamps again, sent the servants to bed, and sprayed the furniture, the carpets and every corner of the room with amber. Then he went to Concepción who was watching with some wonderment. With a gallant air, he bowed gracefully before her, took her hand and kissed it.

"Milady, if your ladyship believes, as I do, that the great farce of the modern world is insipid beyond all reason, join me in this other comedy to which I invite you, for if life be not colored with a tint of fantasy, it becomes tedious rather than entertaining."

"And what am I supposed to answer to that?" asked Concepción, laughing.

"You should answer in this manner. Attend it well: 'It would please me, gallant sir, to join you in this jest. I only ask you, if you esteem me, that the jest never touch on things of the heart, for the heart is a child without malice and does not understand wittiness.' If you said that, I would reply: 'Dispel your fears, beautiful maiden, and if some day you were to believe that everything around you is fiction, jests and lies, that you were the protagonist in a farce and I a phantom of your dreams, I shall not be the one to disillusion you, for I sometimes doubt the very floor I walk on. Yet in the midst of so much fiction, jests and lies I promise you that one thing alone is true, and this is, oh! my sweet enemy, my love which is so great that eyes and words cannot express it. Love, milady, which giving death, is the very life of this heart that adores you.' "

At this point in his narration Contreras asked me for the *bota* which I had been holding while I listened. He took a long drink out of it, and went on: "Since that day neither Concepción nor I have left the orchard. On Sundays a priest comes to say Mass for us and our servants. Concepción is sweet and patient. She knows when I want her with me and when I wish to be alone without my telling her. And we have been living this way for five months without any disturbance until, one fine day, you had to come and break the peace — "

"Don't forget that your contract with the University requires that you spend three months out of every year in America," I said, really alarmed now. "Take Concepción with you if you like. But before the next trip I have some plans for you."

He looked at me with those steely eyes. "To the devil with your plans."

I realized that it would have been foolish of me to insist at that point, so I changed the subject.

"Two things, Captain. The first, will you put me up for the night? I don't want to drive back in the dark."

"Granted."

"The other is that you allow me to ask you a question."

"Granted."

"How do you reconcile all your high and mighty religious ideas with the fact of living this way with a woman . . . a woman who —"

Contreras glared and cut in abruptly.

"That is an affair of which I alone may be the judge."

"Excuse me, I don't want to annoy you."

We were silent a long while. Contreras' thoughts were doubtlessly wandering loftily through space. Mine, less holy than his, followed another road. For the first time I realized that in order to attain my objective, I would have to make a cold-blooded plan, and stick to it mercilessly.

Today I regret this. All that Contreras told me that night, and before and afterwards, I did not truly appreciate and understand. I had my plan, I searched out my objective with cold obstinacy, and I had to ignore what I thought were just blind obsessions on his part. As I write now I feel his presence. I have the impression that he's standing behind me, reading the words that my pen is putting on paper, as though he wanted to stop my using them to justify an attitude which was (I confess it today) ignoble, and even criminal.

My goal was to get Contreras away from that retreat

and restore him to society so that the public might enjoy the living miracle which his presence amongst us meant.

The means employed to get him away seemed justifiable to me at the time. Today they do not. I intended to use Paca Revilla to alienate Contreras from Sylvia. I didn't doubt that Paca would co-operate and do the job.

As for myself, I foresaw no difficulty in conquering Sylvia. After all, I did have the advantage of age over Contreras, plus a certain knavish, unscrupulous charm which a woman like her would probably find attractive.

I was thinking about this when the sound of footsteps made us both turn around. She was coming toward us from the house. She was normally dressed. I mean to say, she was not in costume, as I had feared, like Contreras. Sylvia was pretty enough to prevent any regrets on my part for the project I had in mind. She was slender and her eyes were large and sad. I stood up and Contreras introduced us.

"They are all waiting for you already," Contreras said to her.

Sylvia had great charm. Her body looked young and attractive.

"Every evening at this time," she explained, "we join the servants to recite the Angelus."

CHAPTER SIXTEEN

I WOULD never have suspected that mornings in the country could be all that noisy. For several hours the barking of dogs, the cackling of hens, the rasping of birds, the screeching of roosters and the loud talking of Contreras, combined with the hardness of the bed, made open warfare on my sleep. But when, half beaten, I looked at my watch and saw that it wasn't even seven-thirty, I was furious. And my anger woke me up completely.

I lived at the orchard for five days, an interested witness of the wild race between getting what I wanted and the end of my patience. Which would win? I confess that if I had had to prolong my stay in the country I would have bungled the affair once and for all.

At five-thirty in the morning, Contreras would get up and call for his breakfast and his gun. At six o'clock they brought his hunting dog with whom he held a tremendous conversation under my window shouting exuberant replies to its barks. At seven he went off with the dog. Sylvia got up at eight. At eight-thirty they consented to bring me breakfast in my room.

The mornings were interminable. While Contreras hunted, Sylvia attended to her household duties, and I stayed in my room, writing. Lunch was at twelve. Contreras recounted his morning's adventures without letting anyone else say a word. After lunch, three quarters of an hour's conversation, then the siesta. Everyone but Sylvia and me took a siesta in that house. An hour later Contreras would come back to the sitting room. Sylvia retired and didn't appear again until seven o'clock for supper. Contreras used this time to speak to the foreman, plan irrigation, direct the harvesting, and I don't know what other odds and ends. After supper Contreras and I would sit under the chestnut trees until Sylvia announced that the servants were ready for prayers. After prayers everyone went to bed.

Apart from the day of my arrival when I wasn't given any supper at all, I ate voraciously. The seventeenth century cuisine was not bad, for Contreras had even placed his deft archaic touch on that.

The only thing Contreras could not do was make Sylvia dress in costume. And I noticed that he toned down the pomp of his costume a bit with something of a modern countryman's style, as though to lessen the contrast.

I had to adapt my schedule to the hours kept at the orchard, which to a certain extent helped my plans. During Contreras' siesta I could, without any trouble, talk with Sylvia alone. After supper, while she was busy in the house, I could speak alone with Contreras. And during the day I had a chance to talk with the servants and the country people in the absence of their master. In this way I began to lay my plans.

It was harder with Sylvia than with Contreras. The Captain was like a rocket which, once set off, no one could bring back. But he was like a hand-held rocket that one could point in one direction or another according to the trajectory desired. I was very careful not to irritate him by talking about Sylvia. Any dispute on this score would have angered him and spoiled my future dealings. I managed to attack him on his weakest flank, the flank of wounded self-esteem: Paca Revilla.

"Women," I told him, "are sometimes like fortresses that won't surrender to cannon fire but will open their doors if you knock gently. Why did you run away from New York? In love, as in war, a timely retreat should be purely strategic and not a rout."

Contreras replied that if Paca's attitude were due to virtue or indifference he could understand it, but it was obvious that she was interested in him, for it was she who'd sought him out, and brought him "to the very gates of love." And there she'd stopped, not out of virtue but out of cold calculation! If she'd rejected him it wasn't because she was afraid of a fleeting love affair, but that she was afraid of falling into the snare of a love that was blind, deep and complete. And this was the one thing which he was determined to give and demand: completeness.

Perhaps this eagerness for completeness, he mused, was

the same which had sent him off toward a fierce desire for the beyond, searching and yearning for God.

"Leave God in His place, Captain. We're talking about Paca Revilla."

I went on like this, day after day, fertilizing a ground which was not unwilling to be fertilized.

With Sylvia it wasn't so easy. Sylvia stopped me cold with her serenity, her easy cordiality as a hostess entertaining her husband's friend. The road to intimacy was difficult, especially without so much as friendship to help. I had to remind myself constantly of her past in order to convince myself that my job wasn't impossible.

But this woman is just a whore, I'd tell myself; why am I afraid to tackle her, to worm myself into her confidence?

But the fact is, I did not dare. Sylvia really seemed like a true lady. In those days I knew nothing about her except for what the girls in the Avenida de la Reina Victoria had told me when I went there with Pepe Castejón the night before I came to Toledo. The reader already knows more about her than I did then. To me she was just a prostitute who had managed to bewitch Contreras. I had only one big question, one which Pepe was not able to answer: Did the Captain know about her past or didn't he?

For three days while Contreras took his siesta I had long talks with Sylvia, or, I should say, Concepción. We talked about all kinds of things: about the country, the crops, the relationship between a landowner and his foreman and other thrilling matters. I asked her hundreds of questions about farming, exaggerating my ignorance in order to make her talk. On the third day I was able to make her laugh at my inability to understand how a seed buried in the earth could grow into a watermelon full of sugared water without the need to fertilize the earth with sugar. She laughed so heartily, and I so enjoyed seeing her laugh, that the subtle barrier which stood between us disappeared. This may seem absurd, but nothing shortens a gap between people more than a laugh together.

Nothing could have been more dissimilar than a conversation with Concepción and one with Paca Revilla. Paca was quick, brittle, magnificent at repartee. A chat with her was like conversational badminton where an idea tossed at her was returned with more meaning and wit than it had originally. Sylvia was unable to play this game. She lacked malice. Words for her had no other meanings than those given by the dictionary. She had no secret intentions and did not expect them in others.

When life dragged her into prostitution she quickly learned that it wasn't love but pleasure which was demanded of her for money. And she gave what was asked in exchange for what she received. In Contreras she had found a formula for living without having to sell her body. And she gave him what he wanted in exchange for what she wanted. Instead of that nebulous "something, someone, somewhere" she could answer: "A house, Contreras, Toledo."

Do ut des. I give so that you will give. This ancient and simple formula belonged to Sylvia, I mean Concepción; for what Contreras sought in her, peace, companionship, warmth and friendship, Sylvia could not have given — but Concepción could.

She played the role of Concepción marvelously. That was why my plan was so hard to carry out. I tried to tackle Sylvia — the loose woman — and was brought up short each time by the serenity of Concepción, the lady.

One afternoon it rained as it can only rain in Castilla. It rained à la Captain Contreras: with a downpour and violence, a definite and absolute rain. Daybreak had been cloudy and muggy. The air was as quiet and brooding as a bull about to attack. At midafternoon loud thunder gave the signal for combat; air and water began their tournament over the countryside.

We had to stay indoors. So, in the middle of the afternoon, in the big drawing room, with the postprandial conversation dying on the vine, Concepción went to sit at her embroidery frame, Contreras began to write at the big table, and I started leafing over the books I saw. I came across a curious one and lingered over it. Its title was *Manual of Confessions.* Contreras had marked with red pencil anything that referred to the art of sorcery.

There was also an anthology of verse. Contreras had undoubtedly read it all, for between the pages I found slips of paper scribbled with projects for poems inspired by the earlier writers.

Next to Lope's lines which begin: *Shepherd, who with your flutings amorous,* Contreras had gone on to write a nice little poem, inspired by Fray Luis de León, Juan de la Cruz and Lope de Vega himself.

Shepherd, who with your flutings amorous
Cheer the mountain and the meadow,
Valley, spring and shore,
And shady woods, fluting sonorous!

I know of a gentle ewe lamb
That has lost your light and your path.

Now she wanders blindly
Bleating sadly in the sunny places
Waiting for the stone to wound her
And return her to your pious mountain.
Give her, O Shepherd, your flutings amorous!

"A gentle ewe lamb" . . . Did that refer to Sylvia? Or to his own soul, attached to his body for centuries without being able to fly and unite itself with the Shepherd of the amorous flutings?

"Now she wanders blindly waiting for the stone" . . . The same thought. Was he thinking about Sylvia's waiting for the wounding stone of repentance for her life of sin which would restore her to purity and virtue? Or did it refer to his captive soul waiting for the stone of death which would let him fly to the infinite mountain of holy blessedness?

In any case, I said to myself, *I'll* give her some flutings amorous! No sooner had I murmured this spontaneous hope than I realized the possible results — all I needed at this point was to be influenced by some verses! Verses, furthermore, of Captain Contreras! It was really funny. I laughed.

"What makes you laugh, Cornejo?" Concepción asked.

I felt like a child who is caught doing something

naughty. I made some vague remark and went on reading.

Sylvia went on embroidering. Contreras, serene and
tranquil, was writing at the other end of the room. I
closed my eyes as though to doze; really to have a little
talk with myself.

You have no scruples, I said. Your plans for Concepción could only be conceived by a complete fiend. You
don't like Concepción and you don't even desire her.
You're going after her to rescue Contreras so you can
use him to make money. But you don't like Concepción.
"Hey now wait!" I interrupted myself. "Use any other
argument but not that one — I'm — I'm crazy for that
woman. She attracts me fiercely. But this is a crime too.
Contreras is supposedly your friend, and you are a
wretched excuse for a man. Leave Contreras alone, bury
your evil thoughts about Concepción. Get out of here!"

I got up suddenly, went toward the door.

"Going out in this weather?"

"I'm just going to look at the countryside in the rain,"
I said.

As far as I remember, this was the only time in my life
that I acted mechanically, yet conscious that I was acting
mechanically. I went out into the rain, climbed the hill
and went to where I'd left my car five days before. In
spite of the mud it was easier to drive than I would have
thought. I went without saying goodbye to anyone, without even taking my toothbrush and toilet articles from my
room. I cleared out.

On the road, tied to a tree, curled up under the rain,

was a ewe. My car frightened her, and she leapt up, vainly jumping at the end of the rope. She wanted to get away but she couldn't. My own voice surprised me, saying mechanically: *Give her, O Shepherd, your flutings amorous!*

CHAPTER SEVENTEEN

You're a shameless monster but an attractive one," she said.

"It's too late in the game for flattery, Paca," I said.

"So you've decided to separate this Sylvia from Contreras?"

"Well, that really isn't what I had in mind."

"Then what *is* your plan?"

"To separate Contreras from Sylvia."

Her laugh was delicious. "Isn't that the same thing?"

"No, it isn't the same thing."

"And why do you wish to separate him from Sylvia?"

"Because when she's with him he puts up with his retreat. If she weren't there he couldn't stand it. He'd get out fast and come back to the real world where he'd become rich, powerful, influential, and admired by everyone. His case has been heard of in every country, there isn't a newspaper in the world that hasn't written about it, but he hasn't even begun to exploit it. Contreras is an unexplored gold mine!"

"What a heel you are," she said calmly.

"You're wrong if you think I'm only after his money. I'm going after something else, too, which you wouldn't understand. I'm going to rescue him for society."

"Because of your *great* love for society?"

"No, because of my love for literature."

Sylvia wouldn't have understood any of this. Paca did.

"And what weapons are you going to use?"

"I'm — I'm counting on you."

"On me?"

Although Paca knew perfectly well I was going to say that, she put on an astonished expression.

"I can't help you. If he's in love with Sylvia, that's it."

"Oh, come now! How in the world could he be in love with her? He's in love with you, and you know it."

"Do you really think so?"

"Let's get down to business. Would it amuse you to help me?"

"I think so." She said this in a rather troubled voice.

"Bravo, Paca! bravo! As a reward I won't annoy you any more by telling you that I am, as ever, hopelessly in love with you."

We arrived at the orchard at ten o'clock in the morning. Contreras was out hunting. Concepción came out to receive us. Luigi could take us to the ravine where we could surely find Contreras. But it was far away. If we

would rather wait till he came back she'd be delighted
. . . Paca charmingly assured her that she was a good
walker and liked the country. So she went with Luigi
to look for the Captain.

From the first instant, the first look, I could see that
Concepción was on the defensive. When Paca turned
away with Luigi, she looked her up and down, analyzing
her figure like a man.

"That woman's very elegant."

And she sat down. So did I.

"Jealous, Concepción? That expression on your face
is very becoming. It's . . . it's, I don't know. You're
very pretty, you know."

"Who's that woman? What's she doing here? This
house isn't set up for guests. We live like country people.
There's only room for a man and a woman: the master
and the mistress."

"But Concepción, you aren't married, you haven't the
right — "

She looked at me wonderingly, a strange expression on
her face.

"I don't mean to upset you," I went on to say, "but you
really can't expect — "

Concepción's expression changed as the wonderment
gave way to indignation.

"Just who the devil are you to interfere? Who gave
you the right to speak to a lady like this?"

"All right, all right then, let's stick to the truth."

Concepción lost her control and her manners and began to raise her voice excitedly. They *were* married, she

said, both in the church and in the registry, and I had no right to stir up trouble. She shot a stream of invective at me and, when I saw another in preparation, I said, "Lord, Sylvia, take it easy!"

Concepción opened great astonished eyes at hearing herself called by her *nom de guerre*. The blood which had been driven into her face by anger ran back into her veins leaving an empty pallor on her face. Her hands, which had been gesturing angrily, fell hopelessly to her sides.

"Why did you call me that?" she asked barely audibly.

I lowered my eyes as though ashamed of having gone so far.

"Did you — know me before?" she asked sadly.

I nodded.

"Oh God."

She raised her hands to her face as though she were going to cry. But she didn't. When she took her hands away the pallor was more marked and her gesture had hardened her. She turned and went upstairs. I watched her go and felt rather dazed. Everything had happened so quickly that I took several minutes to put my thoughts in order.

"Listen," Sylvia had said before leaving the room, "don't say anything to Alonso. He doesn't know. Promise me?"

"I swear it."

Paca climbed into the little buggy. Luigi sat proudly beside her, holding the reins.

"Does your master go all this way on foot just to hunt?"

"Yes, señora, every day. He leaves early in the morning with his dog."

"Does he shoot much game?"

"He did at first, señora, but since he always goes to the same place the game has come to know him by now and he knows them and he doesn't shoot much."

They trotted across the fields for a good half hour. The buggy raised a fine dust which hung in the air, marking their passage like smoke from a boat on a still day.

Paca wore a colored scarf around her head to keep her hair in place. A ringlet fell down on her forehead and curled in the breeze. Now and then she made a brusque movement to push it back. She looked very, very beautiful with her delicate nose, her firm lips smiling at the sun and air that caressed her, her brilliant white teeth, her head erect. She did not see the landscape, she was too busy looking for the objective in her mind's eye, her swaggering, brusque, dominating, sure Captain.

Suddenly the land broke away on the left, opening into a deep ravine. There below, solemn and old, glided the river Tagus. Luigi pulled on the reins and the horse stopped. They got down.

"Wait for me here," she said. "I'll look for him."

Paca slid carefully down the bank which overlooked the river. In the distance some women were washing clothes. Some of them, clearly of Moorish descent, carried great pails on one hip while they walked with opposite hand outstretched for balance. On the other bank the ravine swept up until the earth met the first houses hang-

ing over the precipice. The jagged ruins of the Alcázar
of Toledo could be seen clawing at the sky.

In the middle of this scene, forming an integral part
of the landscape like another stone, or an old tree trunk
on the ground, was the figure of Alonso Guillén de Roa y
Contreras. No, it wasn't the swaggering Captain, aggressive and dominating, whom Paca Revilla saw before
her, but a gentle, defeated man. He was so quiet and
absorbed, so close to the earth and so aged that, if the sun
had not been shining brightly in the ravine, she could
have confused him with any one of the fallen trunks
which had once been trees, and which even now lay
among the rocks like old vegetal phantoms.

The Captain was sitting on the ground on a steep
slope. His elbows rested on his knees and his hands on
the head of a cane as though it were a sword. The point
of his chin rested on his hands, and his gaze was on
Toledo.

I wonder if this piece of land has changed much, Paca
asked herself, since the Captain's first life.

Looking around her she realized that everything in
sight from the ancient windmills that drew water for the
Tagus to the old buildings on the opposite hill, from the
Moorish women climbing the slope with their buckets and
baskets to the very songs they were singing might also
have been seen by a quail hunter, or a farmer, or any
passer-by three hundred years ago.

Paca didn't quite know how to approach the meditative
Captain. She sat some distance behind him, armed herself with an arsenal of small pebbles and began to toss

them at her absorbed friend. She had to repeat the shots several times before she perfected her aim. Finally she made a hit between the Captain's shoulder blades. He reacted quickly, jumping to his feet and whirling round, stick in his hand like a sword.

Bravo! thought Paca, Don Alonso hasn't lost his dash.

But Alonso stood as though paralyzed by a vision. It was hard for him to come back to our days, for his thoughts had been leading him on an excursion to the Toledo of Valenzuela, the Toledo of Osorio, of Vilches, of Luigi . . . the Toledo of 1633. He could not understand right away who this woman was, so lightly dressed, who was waving a hand at him and smiling.

"Señor Ungallant, don't you even want to speak to me?"

Contreras stepped forward hesitantly.

"Paca!" he exclaimed. "But it's Paca!"

I had hoped and prayed for this but even I hadn't reckoned how quickly the mercurial and enigmatic man would forget his wife and fall back into Paca's trap.

Then he came toward her like a little child running to join his friends, with his arms open.

"But she has come back to me! My lady has come back to me!" he said while holding her tightly against him. "And perhaps she comes ready to pay the duty she left unpaid with ingratitude!"

"I don't come to pay anything. I have only come to stop a happy, strong, attractive man from burying himself alive — again."

I knocked nervously on her door. From inside, Sylvia asked me who it was.

"It's me — Antonio."

"What do you mean by — "

"It's important. I think you ought to know. Alonso — "

I heard her jump out of bed and look for something to put on.

"What's happened to Alonso? What have you done to him?"

"I'll wait for you downstairs," I said, "in the drawing room."

Sylvia came down seconds afterwards in a dressing gown buttoned up to her throat. It was very pretty and certainly modest enough.

"Alonso has gone."

"Alonso — has gone?" she stammered incredulously.

She was silent a long time. I did not dare look at her face, and took advantage of her daze to light a cigarette.

"With — that woman, of course."

"And in my car!" I exclaimed, pretending indignation.

All she said was, "And that's what's called a lady in high society?"

And Sylvia (she suddenly was no longer Concepción) began to laugh. She came up to me. I thought she was going to strike me, but she only wanted my cigarette. She took it, puffed a few times and sat across from me.

"What are you going to do now?" I asked, as though very concerned for her future.

"Me? Stay here, naturally. I'm not going to chase

him through the streets, crying for him on the corners."

"Of course, I don't suppose he'd mind if you stayed, but . . . what about money?"

"That doesn't worry me. This place is mine. It's in my name."

It was my turn to be astonished.

"What do you mean?"

"Just what you hear."

"Impossible. Alonso doesn't even know how to make out a transfer of property."

"He doesn't, but I do."

She gave a deep drag on the cigarette and threw it away.

"I came here determined to leave my old life, and I made sure I'd be safe no matter what. I wasn't born for — for *that*. Here it seemed that everything in the past was only a dream. Now I'm beginning to think that *this* was the dream. How very nauseating!"

I watched in vain for tears in her eyes. Sylvia did not cry. She had sad eyes and a faraway smile . . . and she was very beautiful in her wretchedness.

"What you haven't realized," she said, looking me in the eyes, "is the harm you've done him, and the harm you will do him — both of you."

"Why do you say *both* of us?"

"Don't be a hypocrite and please don't think I'm that stupid. You've plotted the whole thing and you're a complete heel."

She didn't say it aggressively or insultingly. She said I was a heel in the same way she might have said that the carpet was red or that the night was starry. Worse than an insult, I thought, the sentence was more like an accepted basic fact.

"Only yesterday," I said with a smile, "Paca Revilla told me the same thing. But at least she sweetened it by adding that I was charming."

"Well, I don't think so. I wouldn't be caught dead with you."

And eventually what had to happen, happened: Hadn't I planned it this way?

At my first advances Sylvia gave me a long, cold, look of loathing.

"Not even if I were tied and gagged."

"Don't be a hypocrite, Sylvia. Or do you by chance have to be in love with a man in order to go to bed with him?"

Now she did change her expression. She bit her lower lip in rage. Then she gave me a tremendous slap.

Several days later I was surprised when I woke up in the middle of the night to find that Sylvia, beside me, was crying.

I put my hand on her warm naked shoulder.

"Then you really miss him so much, Sylvia?"

"I'm not crying for him," she whispered softly, "I'm not crying for him. I'm crying for Concepción."

CHAPTER EIGHTEEN

ALONSO'S spirits would sometimes rise to great heights, and then apparently with no cause plunge into a bottomless and shapeless total gloom.

"You're like an elevator in the Empire State Building," Paca told him one day. "But one's never quite sure whether you're going up or down."

"Maybe my soul is making tests, like the airplanes, for a long flight."

"Say no more. Today you're down. I'm leaving — when you're like this no one can stand you."

On his up days Contreras would take the steering wheel from Paca and roar through the countryside at an incredible speed, eating up the miles and shouting snatches of poetry. Strangely, Paca enjoyed this.

One day during a bullfight he leapt into the arena, grabbed a cape from the sword boy and gave the bull three dangerously close verónica passes which won him an ovation. He was arrested, and Paca had to use all her influence to have him released.

"He's a foreign diplomat and you realize that if they take his name it may cost him his career."

They let him go.

There were days when Paca felt imbued with a great tenderness for him. She would have felt it a tragedy to lose him. But she never gave herself to him. She preferred to be a cool yet interested spectator of a little drama that was being acted for her alone.

"I shall conquer this fortress," he told her one day. "I shall tame all those imps you carry inside fighting me and hang them from the yard arm, and then I shall make you totally mine."

"Why do you say totally?"

This disconcerted him.

"Because love, like war, has to be total. Nowadays you have prostituted love. You have clipped its wings. There are lovers who give their bodies but who jealously reserve the liberty to suffer and dream and adore, and there are those who, feeling themselves attracted to the object of their love, prefer to escape rather than to give themselves totally. I don't understand that kind of love."

Paca knew the Captain's character, knew the exact phrase to use at the right moment to distract him, to divert his attention away from his amorous assaults.

"The total love and war you speak of sound cruel. War — "

"War! Everybody used to know why they made war. I remember — "

And Contreras would plunge into the past, vividly making his adventures seem as though they'd happened only yesterday.

Paca would listen to him with absorption, not so much for the incidents he described as for the color he lent his stories. Neither poetry nor music was as moving to her as these tales. He transported her to another world, one in which she sometimes felt she had lived or was living.

Until then all my plans had worked out the way I wished. Paca had played her role to perfection. She had brought Contreras out of that sickly, pseudo-religious, sentimental atmosphere of the orchard. She had kept Sylvia out of his mind by entertaining him, by letting him dream of that fortress he hoped to conquer some day, and which Paca was determined not to yield. For she knew that on the day she gave in to Contreras, the fun of the conquest itself over and self-esteem assuaged, she would cease to have her great appeal for him.

The fear of an angry Sylvia determined not to give up had also disappeared, thanks to my doing. Sylvia, who in the beginning was disgusted with herself, was soon convinced that she should really be feeling this disgust for life itself which had brought her, defenseless, along the paths of degradation. I helped a bit to change the object of her scorn. I was frightened at the possibility of future repentance, the shattering sort which makes people beg forgiveness, weep and tear their hair, get religion, and finally seek redemption.

A fatalistic Sylvia who accepted the role fate had forced her to play would suit my plans much better, and toward this end I paid several visits to her property, the orchard. Nor was it difficult to carry out my purpose. Sylvia, in a sad but human reaction, enjoyed wallowing in more and more filth, undoing the steps which she had thought would bring her to virtue with Contreras. She sank lower and lower each time with a desperate will to cover herself with mud.

In me Sylvia felt she had an accomplice in the same crime. She neither loved nor hated me. But she spoke to me as I doubt she ever spoke to herself. She told me of her life, of her childhood in Villanueva del Río. Her escape to Madrid. Her meeting with Fernando, as I have written it in another chapter. Her first visit to the house where she worked for so long. A girl she knew had taken her there, saying, "It has to be some day, why not now?"

Sylvia told me she could see from the terrace of that house into the lovely garden of the Convent of the Adorers of the Sacred Heart. At evening the nuns would play ball games in the open circle. Then, when the bell rang, they all disappeared like a band of startled swallows. Many evenings Sylvia, who had been watching the nuns play, stayed on when they went in, leaning on the railing, not thinking of anything, until it grew dark. I could imagine her there smiling, with her sad, sad eyes, staring at the inviting garden.

On thinking of this I felt a pang of remorse — a very slight pang, of course — which I tried to kill with the excuse that what I was doing was necessary to my aim of liberating Contreras.

Sylvia spoke to me of meeting Alonso, of the intimacy

which they achieved, of his desire to return to the country, to flee from something unknown to her, but which she understood without knowing; for she too wanted to flee from everything around her.

"I don't know whether he's crazy or not. I just know that he is a man at whose side I was able to be Concepción once again."

I tried to interrupt her when she spoke like this, for I didn't want her to stray; but she'd always end by laughing because she'd let herself be deceived by a dream of impossible virtue. "We who were born to——" (and she spoke the word outright) "will die doing the same. Anyway, he was sort of old, and I missed expert men like you and awkward, ardent boys like Luigi. I've got my personality back now."

On saying this she would laugh and laugh. Each peal of laughter was like a nail driven into my heart, shaming me. For I have never seen sadder eyes, eyes reflecting greater bitterness, than Sylvia's when she threw back her head, laughing and laughing.

CHAPTER NINETEEN

THE DATE for Contreras' stage appearance was now set. My expert publicity had raised such expectations that no one was talking of anything else in all Spain. Long lines formed at the box office for tickets to the three lectures on Love, Art and War respectively, which the Captain was to deliver on three successive days. Dr. Yuste had announced that he'd be back in the country in time to be present at the first one. Paca Revilla, Castejón, Molludo, the Robledos, Dorita Rivas, Morales the Commissioner, even Sylvia, and anyone else who had known the Captain, were besieged with requests for tickets regardless of price. Although at first I'd refused to have the lectures broadcast so as not to reduce the sale of tickets, the demand was so great that I finally gave the exclusive — and very expensive — rights to one company for a rebroadcast.

I was in seventh heaven.

Three days before the first of the lectures Contreras came up with a strange fancy.

"I am curious to see my bedroom."

He wanted to drive out to the Almudena Cemetery to see the iron casket where he had slept for nearly three centuries. There was nothing wrong with this: I even decided that it might not be a bad theatrical touch to place the casket near the speaker's rostrum.

We went in the car to the cemetery gates and crossed the border that separates the land of the living from that of the defunct. The land of the dead was green, flowering and pleasant. Old trees with thick trunks lent shade to the many paths that crossed the cemetery and tapering cypresses pointed skyward as though they were indicating the way.

First we crossed the section for the rich. Little temples with their spires worked in stone like tiny cathedrals, family vaults with the names carved on the marble, many of them larger and more ornate than the humble sepulcher of Christ under the church built by Philip II in Jerusalem. Contreras stopped before a white marble angel. It had one hand stretched toward a catafalque and the other on its lips, asking for silence. A woman in black marble lay prostrate over the catafalque, weeping motionless across time.

After a brief transition that was an unsuccessful imitation of luxury, we passed simpler, more modest vaults, and were soon in the middle-class section. Was this arrangement casual, or was this dividing of the cemetery an attempt to forget that "there all lordly rights will end and be consumed"? The Captain, with his cane held like a sword, peered into every path and crossway between the tombs.

He went removing withered flowers and the dust that covered the inscriptions with his cane. The graves, the size of a child's mattress, were now limited to a slab of stone or marble with a cross in front, and some of the fancier ones had a sort of alabaster shroud, nearly transparent, draped over the arms of the cross.

One inscription said:

*She sinned much . . . She loved much . . . She wept much
Forgive her, Lord!*

Another said:

*Adolfo Montero
Went to rest in the Lord,
15 years of age.
His mother will remember him eternally.*

Farther away the mother was resting too.

I thought that this boy might be myself dead as a child; my mother would not have given me an inscription like that. The idea displeased me and I managed to dismiss it. I turned away to Contreras who was sniffing and poking about among the dead.

We came into a wide semicircle where the niches stood against the wall. Some had inscriptions, a name, a date. Some had only a wooden cross leaning against the little ledge where the inhabitants rotted. Some just had a cross marked in chalk. This was the poor quarter of the dead. The great wall, riddled with niches, looked like an apartment house from which the façade had been removed, revealing the narrow squares of rooms, or a heap of stage sets under which the actors were asleep. At this spot the Captain looked all around him quickly. His nostrils flared as though he were sniffing something. He turned around several times, then went toward a part of the wall where a mound of building material indicated that the cemetery was about to be enlarged.

He climbed over a pile of bricks and found the iron casket half covered with earth. I helped him dig it out with a spade that was there. Some spiders and small insects like dwarf beetles ran out.

"Ah, rascals!" shouted Contreras, "so you miss me, eh?"

All this repelled me. It unnerved me.

Noticing my discomfort, he dedicated himself to squashing them with the end of his cane, accompanying each demise with outlandish exclamations.

"Ah, thief! Son of a whore! Go sleep with Satan!"

Upon saying this he would squash it.

"Villain! You will keep company in hell with many who sleep here!"

"Come on, Contreras, that's enough. I find it all in rather bad taste. Let's go."

He roared with laughter.

"This isn't a place to laugh. Come on, man, let's go!"

I started to leave, but he caught me with the crook of his cane and pushed me onto the pile of bricks.

"Is Mr. Scribbler scared, by chance? Sit down, my fastidious friend."

Then he lowered his voice.

"Señor Cornejo, you're afraid and you don't know why. Well, I'll have to tell you. You're afraid of the Noseless One, aren't you? I have seen her at a thousand crossways with her sickle ready to reap me. If she got too near me, I would play a trick on her and attack the very ones who were pushing her toward me. One fears the unknown. And so, my dear impresario, my protector, in payment for the many services I have received at your hands, I, Captain Alonso Guillén de Roa y Contreras, will now introduce her to you."

I tried to force a little laugh and said as calmly as I could, "Look, Captain Alonso, I'm in a hurry. I have other things to do, so I shall leave you cracking your little jokes and go."

He gave a loud cry that chilled my blood.

"Are you mad — all the paths out of here are taken by the Noseless One! Back, idiot, back!"

I stopped, stupidly, then I reacted and tried to run away.

Contreras faced the niches, shouting: "I conjure whoever is there to bar this idiot's way! You —" he pointed to a niche with a chalk cross — "order them all. Come, my officers, and at him!"

At that moment a sudden breeze stirred the high foliage of the cypresses, which swayed solemnly as though responding to his conjury. I was paralyzed, mute with terror, for in that moment I was aware of some fleeting gusts of wind and strange presences around me. I had the feeling that thousands of eyes were fixed on me. I felt my face go pale and the hair rise on my temples, and

the blood stop in my veins. I turned around and then
jumped backward because I saw — what did I see? Perhaps no more than a rhododendron rocking in the breeze.

When my limbs obeyed me I ran back, cowardly and
trembling, and threw my arms around Contreras' legs.
I find the telling of this whole episode rather humiliating
but my heart was beating so fast it was difficult to
breathe. I think I partly fell to the ground and had my
arms round one of Contreras' legs. He was sitting on the
pile of bricks and drew me to him, warmly and teasingly.

"Ah, Señor Antonio Cornejo, calm your soul. And
don't think it was a joke, my conjury of these people who
live here to come to my aid. It was very true. I have
become fond of you and it rends my soul to see how
blindly and wildly you go about the world. Calm yourself, I say. There is nothing to be afraid of in milady,
the Noseless One, when, at the end of the reckoning, it is
she, and no other, who will give you the last embrace."

I didn't dare look at him. He was speaking now in
a low and highly emotional tone. Was he indeed mad as
a loon?

"You remain, without wishing to penetrate the mystery, on the surface of things. You have resolved the little
problems of health and body hygiene, but you forget
the more important health of the soul. You have discovered how to conquer the distances of the earth, but you
don't worry about reserving a ticket for the last and
most important of journeys.

"You have resolved the problems of matter, which is
good and just in itself and pleasing to God, but you have

forgotten that you have a spirit which you must care for and water if it is to have flowers and fruit, like the wild flowers before they are scythed by the Noseless One. For Death, when she reaps lives, does not keep them for herself, but takes them to the great Gardener. If He sees that they are in bloom he makes nosegays which He keeps beside Him, enjoying their scent for all eternity. But if they are withered He puts them aside with the thorns and the weeds because their presence is not pleasing to Him. This business of our flowering is the *only* business which matters in the long run. So, you see, one should not be an enemy of the Noseless One, but be able to say like me: 'Wait, milady, don't reap this wretched plant, for it has not quite blossomed yet.' "

After saying this the Captain could not go on because suddenly tears drowned his voice.

CHAPTER TWENTY

VILLA ARDOSA. Madrid. A midnight in summer. Boyish old men with their girl friends. The Minister at one table. From time to time a yawn, a bit of gin, a wise-crack, a kiss. Rumbas, mambos, maracas. ("Have you seen Charito? How she's aged!") Porcelain smiles.

"We shouldn't speak to Molludo tonight. He's dancing with a very dubious blonde."

"That's ridiculous. He's seen us. We know that he knows we've seen him. It would be absurd not to speak to him."

"It doesn't matter. One must observe the rules."

A Negro hits a large collection of cymbals and drums with a savage rhythm. Legs and arms on springs jerk from the rubber bodies, epileptically following the rhythm.

"Adolfo's wife told me she was so disappointed that he could only spend three days with the family in San

Sebastian this summer, because he just couldn't leave the office."

"So what?"

"Look at him out there dancing with his office — a platinum blonde office!"

Contreras was at a table near the orchestra with Paca Revilla, Pepe Castejón and Anita Samper. At the other end of the room two of Sylvia's ex-roommates drank *crème de menthe*, hoping that someone would ask them to dance and start their evening's business. In one corner Dorita Rivas flirted with an American tourist.

Everybody worked at enjoying himself in this outdoor club, breathing in the few hours of the night when the summer fire of Madrid abated. Only Contreras felt uncomfortable. People began to recognize him, and couples danced near so that they could see him better. He looked slightly older and thinner, but extremely distinguished. As I approached his table I imagined the effect he would have on his audience during the lectures that were to start tomorrow night. Sunburned as he was, the width of his brow emphasized by the shining silver at his temples, his gray eyes ablaze with fire when he spoke, his features sharpened and refined by his recent loss of weight, and with his athletic body, Contreras, I was sure, would make quite an impression.

He spoke to me cordially enough, but looked into my eyes so intently that I began to wonder if someone had insinuated something about my frequent visits to Sylvia in the orchard. Hours later I discovered that my suspicions were unfounded. He seemed not exactly sad, but far away. Paca frequently leaned toward him and said something as though to bring him back to reality.

The orchestra began a rumba. The gluey, fluting voice of the band leader began a song. I asked Anita Samper to dance while Castejón took Dorita Rivas out on the floor.

Contreras couldn't repress his amazement at seeing Castejón, in whom he always saw his distinguished ancestor the Viceroy of Sicily, writhing his shoulders and hips so ridiculously to that African music.

Paca put her hand on the Captain's. Her gesture was sweet but her voice was less so.

"What's the matter with you? You seem to be going out of your way to show everybody that you aren't having a good time with me."

Contreras was silent a moment, then said, "Excuse me, I am obeying your rules the way you taught me to."

"But not to the point where you have to be aloof with me. I'd — I'd do anything to see you happy. *Anything.*"

He made a gesture of surprise.

"Do you mean that, Paca?" he said slowly. "Really?"

"Yes."

"At last!"

Contreras took both her hands and pressed them tightly, warmly.

"I had begun to doubt whether this fortress had a heart," he said.

Paca's eyes glistened as though wet with unshed tears. She passed her hand over her forehead as though to push back the curl that was bothering her.

When the rumba was over we returned to our table. Contreras, buoyant, invited us all to champagne. He drank more than usual.

"Let's go," he said several times to Paca. "The rest of them may stay if they wish."

"No," she answered furiously. Her eyes shot daggers at him for his lack of discretion. "It's still early."

The orchestra began to play a mambo. It sounded like pots and pans falling on a set of crockery to Alonso.

"Music hasn't progressed much since your time, has it, Contreras?" Castejón asked him jokingly.

"Neither music nor anything else," he growled. "Art has prostituted itself, it has sold itself for money."

"You aren't fair in that," replied Pepe. "On what do you base your statement?"

"Now don't start talking about serious things," Paca cut in uneasily. "Alonso, dance with me, will you?"

But Alonso didn't hear her.

"The prostitution of art would not have major importance if it only meant the decadence of painting, writing and sculpture, but my God — "

"When you get him started nobody can stop him," laughed Paca, preparing to suffer.

" — do you think it is pure coincidence that values all over the world have fallen down? Today the aristocracy imitate the crude and the vulgar in their wit and their vocabulary. The wise men and philosophers boast of being unbelievers, thus imitating the uneducated. And there is a reason for this crumbling and the vulgarization of customs and the loss of faith. That reason is clear as air: it is that in my day man rowed with two oars but today with only one."

Paca laughed. "That reason is so clear that none of us has understood it!"

Contreras did not laugh. His eyes burned with a fever. At nearby tables people had stopped talking and were listening to our conversation. Some had even brought their chairs quite openly to our table, enlarging our group.

"Humanity is a great galley sailing over the sea of life. In order to move forward the galley needs two groups of oarsmen. Those seated to port understand only the things of the spirit. Those at starboard know only material things. When the two groups row in unison the ship glides ahead perfectly. This is progress. If only one group of oarsmen works, the ship turns around and around; this is stagnation. Believe me, humanity today is rowing with the oar of materialism only."

There was a murmur at these words. This time Paca didn't ask him to dance. A few couples — with frozen smiles — danced to the music which was now slow and intimate. The group at our table had increased by ten or twelve people. Most of them didn't understand what was being said, but listened curiously, entertained by the personality of this man about whom they had heard so much.

"Very well," said somebody harshly, "you have posed the problem. Now give us the solution."

"Row with two oars, by Christ, row with two oars!"

Clearly Contreras had not chosen the best spot in the

world for presenting his theories. When Paca saw him getting worked up she began to feel uncomfortable. Uncomfortable for him, because she noticed the giggles and remarks and nudges of those who had drawn near, attracted by the power of his voice.

"He's a fantastic madman," one said. Another whispered that he was a charlatan hired by me to publicize the lectures. She felt uncomfortable for her own sake too. At the beginning of the evening, she'd been weak and unexpectedly sentimental enough to say that she'd do anything to see him happy. And there had been so much tenderness and gratitude, so much emotion in his look and in the warmth with which he pressed her hands, that Paca believed for the first time that she might be able to love this man "totally."

Now she was regretting her remark. He acted like a clod, she was thinking, insisting so loudly that we leave alone. He might as well have announced over the orchestra's microphone that I was going to go to bed with him!

But Paca wasn't being honest with herself. What really hurt her was that she thought Contreras was making himself ridiculous. And her, too, by reflection. "Your Captain is *very* attractive," she had said months before when she first met him. And he really was, she thought, as though to excuse herself. Now everybody laughed at him. How many took him seriously? Actually, when you came right down to it, Contreras was a ridiculous figure.

Paca was unable to conceal a certain brusqueness toward the Captain. He was stunned. What had he done to deserve this tone of voice and glacial look from the woman who had just said she would do anything to make him happy? Had he said something improper? Had he failed in one of those modern formulas which — Good Lord — he would never be able to learn? Awkwardly, he tried to make it up by reciting a little poem about "angry eyes being none the less beautiful in their anger."

But she cut him short by saying coldly, "Don't be a fool!"

Then turning to Castejón, she said, "Do you want to dance, Pepe?"

Afterwards she regretted her coldness. Contreras didn't deserve that. How stupidly you're acting, Paca Revilla! she said to herself. At the end of the party try to be pleasanter. *Try!*

But Contreras couldn't read her thoughts, only what her lips said and her eyes insinuated, and he felt like a child who has been cruelly punished by having his hands slapped when his hands were about to do a good deed. In many of his reactions, Contreras was still a child and his expression of surprise, pain and incredulity was so intense that I thought he was going to burst into tears right there.

And then something fatal happened to start off a chain of incidents. It seems that one of the waiters, upon hearing the Captain's lecture, and seeing him surrounded by a crowd, went to the owner who asked:

"Why aren't the people dancing?"

"A drunk's got them away from their tables with some junk about the soul."

"Tell the bandleader to get them dancing, and quick. I don't care how he does it."

The bandleader gave instructions to his boys, who nodded, and at the end of the next chorus they began to chant in rhythm the names of those who weren't dancing, beginning with old Molludo:

> *Who isn't dancing la conga?*
> *Don Cosme Molludo's not dancing la conga!*
> *Make him get up and dance,*
> *Ay, niña, la conga!*

He laughed delightedly at hearing his name called, and took his girl to join the conga line. The system worked, and the floor soon filled up with those whose names were called. The more bashful started to dance before their names could be called while the disdainful ones didn't dance, waiting to hear their names. The waiters went around the tables asking the names of the customers they didn't know, and took these to the leader who read them over the microphone.

In the meantime Contreras stayed in a daze. He stared appalled at Paca contorting herself in that frivolous way, dancing that absurd, decadent thing with Castejón as though nothing had happened, as though she didn't know that his heart was torn, bleeding with pain and shame and bewilderment.

Alonso made an angry gesture even before the leader began to chant:

> *Who isn't dancing la conga?*
> *El capitán Contreras!*
> *El capitán Contreras . . .*

It happened very quickly. Like superimposed photographs, I saw first the Negro singer's face with his watermelon smile open from ear to ear. I saw Contreras make an angry grimace. Then, incredibly, he had a knife in his hands. I saw the knife flash out of his fingers and saw the Negro duck quickly. And the knife was quivering in the wood of the big bongo drum.

A noise was heard like *clock!* but the band went on playing. Only a very few people were aware of what had happened. It was a question of seconds. Then a waiter came up to us.

"Sir, it is urgent," he said to Contreras, "the telephone."

He got up and I followed behind him. As he stepped behind the cypress hedge that shut off the dancing area, a courteous voice said, "This way, sir."

As Contreras turned, an iron fist came out of the darkness and slammed savagely onto the point of his chin.

Paca Revilla came up at exactly that minute.

Contreras staggered and crashed down on his back full length at Paca's feet. A thread of blood trickled from his lips.

Paca gave a cry, but she stayed frozen there, making no move to go to his inert form.

Three huge men came up to me.

"Nothing's happened, understand? Get him out of here — we don't want any scandal."

These were the bouncers. One of them rubbed his fist which was already swelling and turning blue. They themselves helped us carry Contreras, unconscious, to the car.

"Is he hurt?" I asked Castejón, who was feeling the

Captain's head, which had struck hard against the pavement.

"No, I don't think so."

And we put him in the back seat of the car.

"Anita and I are leaving too," said Paca. "We'll get a taxi."

We left Villa Ardosa behind with its boyish old men and its distinguished married couples, light and shade of a summer's night in Madrid.

CHAPTER TWENTY-ONE

CONTRERAS regained consciousness even before the motor had started.

"That man had a good fist," he breathed. "By the wounds of God he had a good fist!"

I was driving and Pepe Castejón was in back with the Captain, who seemed suddenly completely all right.

"With men like him we wouldn't have lost the Mahometa, for all our men were hungry or wounded and weak. Son of my mother, but that rascal has a good fist!"

"How do you feel?"

"I? I couldn't be better. I only regret falling down like a buffalo before I could see how you gentlemen dealt with that giant. I regret not having seen you, Señor Marqués, fight in my defense, for surely a person like you who carries in his veins the blood of my master Don Lorenzo Suárez de Figueroa y Córdoba must have fought well."

Pepe Castejón took these words very seriously. In the rear-view mirror I saw him coloring like a student.

"Your ancestor, Don Lorenzo, would rather have lost his life," said Contreras slowly, "than lose a friend."

"Be quiet, Alonso," I said sharply. "Between the punch you got and your rantings you'll have a concussion."

Contreras put his hand to his forehead suddenly. He tried to laugh and pass it off, but then he said, "It does hurt . . . it hurts, all right. It's as though all the devils were dancing between my temples."

But then he shook his head and seemed fine.

We came to the outskirts of town.

"And Paca? Have you left her alone back there?"

"She — she said she'd rather take a taxi," I stammered. "It'd have been a bit rough for her to have got mixed up in that scandal, understand?"

"No," he said, "I do not understand."

Then, after a while, he asked, "Where are we going?"

"Home, of course, to sleep."

"I have a whim. Gentlemen, the night is young. I'm not sleepy. I suggest a walk through the cemetery. There isn't a pleasanter, cooler garden in all Madrid."

"You're crazy! I've got to get some sleep."

We let Pepe Castejón out in front of his house. He said to Contreras, "If I were able to make a visit to your century the way you've done to ours, then I'd be a man! Here, now, I'm no more than the end of my line."

He stayed on the sidewalk waiting for us to drive off. His hair, half blond and half gray, balding in front; his clear almost feminine eyes with that peculiar expression of absent-mindedness and sadness; his height and slenderness . . . all of this made him look like a gentleman, in spite of the shabby cloth of his jacket and the darns in his shirt under his tie.

Fortunately I drove away before he could really hear the terrible reply bellowed out by Contreras: "It isn't true that you'd have been better than you are now! There isn't the material for it, Señor Marqués, there isn't the material for it!"

Contreras said this leaning back out the window with great shouting and gestures. Pepe couldn't hear him but stood on the sidewalk watching him just the same.

I remarked, "You're out to lose all your friends, aren't you?"

"My friends! Show me the wounds they have earned in my defense!"

I didn't want to answer just then. Only when I left him in his house I said as pleasantly and sincerely as I could, "You betrayed Yuste in New York by leaving on the day of the banquet in his honor, even though you owe your life to him. You've insulted Castejón. Paca Revilla is getting fed up with your behavior. You abandoned Concepción, who was faithful to you. If you lose everyone who's fond of you, what's left?"

He looked at me with a pained expression — especially at the mention of Concepción's name — as though he wanted to protest. But he only said, "I find myself a stranger among my own. You are all strangers to me!"

I said good night to him, begging him to get some rest;

the next day he would have to be in full possession of his faculties for the great event of the first lecture.

"My friend," he said casually, "you may say goodbye to that idea. Tomorrow there will be no lecture."

I thought he was joking.

"Everything I had to say I have already said, and no one has listened to me."

I realized the terrible fact that he was in deadly earnest.

"Of course you'll speak! The tickets are sold . . . We're sold out, the whole theater!"

Contreras smiled, and looked me up and down as though wondering which one of my bones it would be most fun to break first. I stood my ground. I had staked everything on those lectures: my career, my money and my friends.

"Contreras," I said between clenched teeth, "you're going through with this thing! You hear me? Going through with it!"

"I shall not speak," he repeated calmly, enjoying the anger that sprang from my eyes. The blood rushed to my face. It was all I could do to keep from strangling him.

But then I thought: Better wait, don't insist too much now with the stubborn jackass, but wait until tomorrow when Paca Revilla, with her influence over him, could talk him out of this stupid idea.

"We'll talk tomorrow, Alonso." I tried to say it genially, though my body was trembling. "Maybe things'll look differently to you."

"I won't speak," he muttered for the last time.

He turned his back on me.

It was only then that I noticed the wound on the back of his head where he had fallen to the pavement. Castejón had not noticed it.

"But Alonso, you're hurt!"

I washed off the dry blood with extreme care so as not to make it bleed again. I cut the hair around the wound to prevent infection, and I saw that it wasn't too deep, apparently just a superficial cut.

"You ought to go to bed now and rest."

I bandaged him. He didn't even thank me.

When I left Contreras the night was still young, as he had said. The dance, the music, Paca's annoyance, the bouncer incident, the Captain's unjust words to Pepe Castejón, and, above all, the threat that he wouldn't speak tomorrow, had awakened me to such a point that I couldn't have slept even had I gone to bed.

I put down the top of the car, turned on the radio and glided through the streets aimlessly. The light from the incandescent lamps of some street workers was the only light in the dark, sleeping city. Contreras' imps put the idea and desire to see Sylvia in my brain. I relaxed and let myself be taken wherever the imps wished. They wanted to take me to Toledo.

While I drove, Contreras' refusal to speak pounded in my brain. But I managed to shake off my worries by thinking of Sylvia asleep in her bed at the orchard, lying there not knowing that I was speeding to her side.

I was not with Contreras later that night, so of course

I can't be sure what impulses made him act as he did. But it isn't difficult to imagine. He was tormented by the desire to go away. Everything around him had become insufferable. He saw only one island of peace in his path: Concepción. At her side God beckoned. With that marvelous, childlike facility of his to switch his feelings, he suddenly felt that he must have her and only her.

He would go to her, drop humbly to his knees before her, and say, "Lady, I have sinned unpardonably against heaven and against you. But I do not come back like the Prodigal with empty hands. I bring in one hand a staff for you to lean on. The other hand is extended that I may lean on you. Has not our union been blessed before the altar? Then let us face life together."

Yes, this is what he must do — go to her like a good and true man, live a virtuous life at her side for the days remaining to him to make up for his having betrayed her.

So *now*, when I look back on it, it was logical that Contreras would head for the orchard after his various defeats and humiliations. But *then*, at the time, it hadn't occurred to me, and when it happened it was like a nightmare.

When Sylvia's sudden movement next to me woke me up, when I opened my eyes and saw her lying there on the bed, her eyes wide with terror, when I heard Contreras' voice call: "Concepción!"

Naked, I leapt to the window. I measured the distance. I saw that it would be impossible to jump. I quickly put on my robe and dropped a pistol into one of its pockets. I went to the door, drew the bolt, and stepped into a corner to wait.

Contreras took ten seconds to pound up the stairs and reach the door, but they seemed like an eternity. Sylvia was very pale as she clutched at the sheet that covered her. The door opened softly as though not to startle a sleeping person. Contreras came in on tiptoe, smiling.

"But you're not asleep," he said gently.

Then he saw me.

He went rigid and his smile became so fixed that without actually moving any facial muscles it somehow was transformed into the grimace of a maniac. Everything now seemed to happen in unbearably slow motion because of the lucidity and tension of all my faculties in that instant. He had his head bandaged the way I had left it several hours before, and was unarmed except for his cane. From his chest came not a voice, but the snarl of a wild animal. He glanced at my hand in my pocket and obviously knew I had the pistol. Then he looked me in the eyes and drew up as proudly as a fighting cock. Fleeting sparks passed across his eyes — was it the memory of Captain Pedro Xaraba del Castillo who had attacked Isabel in his house so very long ago?

He was not pale but flushed; his smile was ghastly. The gleam in his eyes seemed to be Sicily, his adulterous wife surprised, and he "who was his friend but now hers" protecting himself, the coward, with a feather pillow for a shield.

"One step more and I shoot!"

Why did I say that? Contreras hadn't moved. Mine was the first voice to be heard in that scene. Even though it was mine I felt reinforced upon hearing it, as if it were the presence of an ally. Contreras looked first at my eyes and at the bulge of the gun under the silk and then at my eyes again. If it were necessary to shoot, I would.

"You're surprised at seeing me here," I said haltingly. "Well, you shouldn't be. You don't know what this woman is — you don't even know her name. Get out of here and we'll avoid a tragedy."

Sylvia slid fearfully out of bed and went to the corner farthest from Contreras. He kept looking at the gun, and I knew that he might jump at me at any time, forcing me to do what, at all costs, I wanted to avoid.

"Does it surprise you to find another man in your bed? You fool! Do you think that all the men who've used her body would fit in this room, or even in the whole house?"

I saw that I had shot with a bullet surer than the gun's. Contreras sagged as though the bullet had found its mark. I shot again.

"Do you think she minds my saying this? She's hard as nails, Contreras, hard like any other whore. Ask her yourself, go on, ask her!"

Sylvia threw her head back and looked at the Captain while moving near me. Contreras' eyes had a glazed benumbed look, and his head kept moving back and forth stupidly in disbelief.

Sylvia put her hand on my arm as though to lean on it. Then suddenly, treacherously, she flung her arms around me, throwing all the weight of her body against the hand that held the gun.

"Now, Alonso," she cried, "now!"

If this were fiction, here is what obviously would have happened next: Contreras, the man of action, would have leapt forward, felled me with one blow of his great fists, and grabbing his beloved he would have fled off to one of his cherished Mediterranean islands, there to live in tranquil bliss the rest of his days. But those are not the facts.

If he'd thrown himself on me at that moment he could have disarmed me easily. But he didn't. I pushed Sylvia to the floor, jerked the gun out of my pocket, and kept it leveled at Contreras' heart. He hadn't moved. He let the cane fall from his hands, dropped his head on his chest, and stood there quietly like a tired animal.

Keeping my distance and still aiming the gun at him, I backed out of the room, closed the door and fled from the orchard. I did not lose control of my nerves until hours later.

Behind that door Captain Alonso remained on his feet, his chin resting on his chest and his arms limply at his sides; his feet were planted apart to keep his balance. His mouth was half open and he moved his chin as though he were chewing. Sylvia had dragged herself across the floor to him and threw her arms around his legs, not daring to lift her eyes to his.

What had happened to him? Was it the physical blow of the night before? Or the blow of learning about the woman? Or just the culmination of all his disillusionment hitting him at once?

He was surprised that he was able to breathe and see and that his legs obeyed him. There at his feet, like one more vision, was a stuffed figure, a phantom that was sobbing. He put his hands to his face as though to keep in the many thoughts that were flooding his brain. He must be waking up from the potions which Valenzuela and Luigi had given him, the effects were wearing off. Now he remembered everything well. He had slept the number of days foreseen by his protectors. They had disguised him so that he might escape from Osorio. "It has to be done. Quickly! There's no time to lose . . ."

"I am thirsty," he said.

That bundle at his feet got up slowly and slipped out the door. Contreras reeled, and leaning against the wall, he lurched out of the room. He found himself in a larger one. Who had brought him here? This must be the mansion of his patron, the Count of Monterrey who had acceded to Luigi's pleas to offer him a refuge, for even though he had been accused of being King of the Moors, there were still gentlemen to support him, knowing of his services to His Majesty.

The woman brought him a glass of water. He gulped it gratefully.

She was wearing a transparent tunic that scarcely covered her shoulders but reached to her feet. The nails on her feet and hands were painted in the Oriental fashion. Doubtless she was a Moor who had been sent to serve him.

Valenzuela's magic had not disappeared. He had the sensation that he was floating. The walls and the furniture, even that woman who smiled at him although her eyes were full of tears, came before his eyes only to be blotted out. He was ready to fall, but he held himself up with a supreme effort. He felt so weak, but he had to escape! The followers of Osorio must not suspect the trick he had played them.

"I have to escape." He tried to move, but as he did the glass fell from his hands and crashed on the floor. At the same time he collapsed like a wounded bull in the arena.

Sylvia rushed to him.

"Alonso, Alonso, what's the matter?"

Upon hearing her cries Luigi and the other servants came in. They lifted their master off the floor and laid him on a sofa. Contreras looked unseeingly at them, then closed his eyes.

"Who are you, woman, and why do you cry?"

"You have a fever — you're delirious! Alonso, Alonso, it's I, Sylvia!"

Contreras stared at her a long time.

"Sylvia . . . Sylvia? I don't know who you are."

"I'm not Sylvia!" She was sobbing now. "Alonso, look at me! Wake up! I'm Concepción."

He instinctively withdrew the hand she held. Sylvia cried out in anguish.

"Forgive me! Pray God to give you time to forgive me — don't go, don't go without forgiving me!"

Contreras put his hand on her head and caressed it.

"I don't know who you are, good woman, nor why you weep. But there is no force now that can delay me. I must set sail today, for my life, my honor and my service to the King depend on it."

A servant leaned toward Sylvia. "Don't make him talk. It's bad for him."

"Knave, villain!" cried Contreras. "How dare you? I don't know how many days I have been under a spell without being able to speak. Today I must speak even though I burst . . ." He softened his voice to add: "Tell me, woman, or lady, for I know not who you are or the cause of your sorrow."

And as though confessing to a priest, Sylvia put her lips to his ear, and, as the tears rained down her cheeks, she poured out her heart to him, the depth of her love, the depth of her sorrow. From time to time he pressed her hand with his as she talked.

Then his forehead and temples began to sweat, his lips parched, and for a while he seemed to sink into a coma. The servants knelt down and started to pray.

Then with sudden lucidity he murmured: "Lady, I must set sail. But believe that if your sins have separated you and your love they have united you, with the mercy of God. May this be a consolation to you, for your tears are a clear sign that wherever he is, he still has power to move your heart. Look for him, look without resting, and if you do not find him among men you will find him one day among those who were once men. Retire where the seed that he planted may blossom in your heart, for it would be a great pity were the winds to blow it away.

"When you retire say to those who ask you where you are going: 'To serve another King, for I am tired.' And when it is time for you to awaken you will not have to say to the Noseless One, as I, a sinner, have so often said, 'Wait, milady. Do not reap this wretched plant, it has not blossomed yet.' "

Sylvia, kneeling beside the lifeless body of Contreras, wept no more.

The servants cried. Luigi cried, sobbing like a child. But Sylvia did not weep, for she saw that her life had blossomed before it was reaped.

EDITOR'S NOTE

Seated at his desk, Antonio Cornejo, "journalist, bachelor, ambitious, and anything but a fool," as he described himself, was engaged in that difficultly pleasant task of inscribing dedications to critics and friends in the first copies of his book just off the press — the book you have just read. He did not know that the few books on his table would be the only ones to reach circulation, for the rest of the edition was to be confiscated by Court Order a few hours later.

He was so absorbed in his work that he did not hear the doorbell ring, nor did he notice that two men had come into his study and were silently looking over his shoulder.

"María!" he called, "take these books out of here and have them delivered."

He started to get up. And then he saw the two men.

"Morales!" he managed to say. "How are you?"

"My colleague, Inspector Arias."

Cornejo swallowed and cleared his throat casually. "A pleasure, Señor Arias. Sit down, please."

"Thank you," Arias said dryly without accepting the chair.

"Our visit will be very short," explained Morales.

Cornejo swallowed again.

"You understand, Cornejo, how we dislike doing this. We've come to arrest you."

Cornejo made a brief gesture of surprise. He lit a cigarette and took a puff. "Have you a warrant?"

Arias put his hand into an inside pocket, took out his wallet and held out the warrant to Cornejo. He did not take it.

"All right. That's all right. And . . ." Cornejo took another puff. "May I know what I am accused of?"

"Yes, of course. You are accused of various crimes, among them . . . murder."

Cornejo turned pale. He had to lean on the table.

Arias became impatient. Morales went up to the reporter.

"Come on, Cornejo, let's not waste time."

One month before the Captain's final adventure Cornejo had hurriedly delivered the manuscript of his book to the press, hoping that it could be sold in the lobby of the Lara Theater before and after Contreras' lectures. However, there wasn't enough time to publish the book before that date, and this allowed Cornejo to add, two days after the last incident, the ending of his book, which you have just read. Impressed by the publicity of the latest events, which would obviously help the sale, the publishers took only two days to deliver the first copies to the author. Forty-eight hours after that Inspector Morales had already studied them and convinced Francisca "Paca" Revilla, Countess of Alcedo, that she should make a complaint of libel against the author as the only means of legally banning the book and its revealing remarks about her. Cornejo had already distributed the first copies before the ban became effective.

The few lucky ones who received those copies have kept them as a real bibliographical curiosity; not for their literary merit, which is highly debatable, but for the extraordinary furor they created. The fact that the rest of the edition was withheld from the public made those few copies collectors' items and extremely valuable.

Now our publishing firm herewith makes the edition available exactly as it was written by its author. This Editor's Note has been added in accordance with the conditions imposed by the authorities upon their consenting to lift the ban that has been in effect for two years.

The results which Morales arrived at from reading the book and from his personal investigations are amply recorded in a detailed report made by the Inspector for his superiors.

Morales begins by stating baldly that Contreras was a fake, that in reality he was one Alfredo Tarranco, native of Tomillar de la Cuesta, a village in the Province of Valladolid, who left home at the age of thirteen to join a company of strolling players who were passing through.

This Tarranco went to Brazil where he became an actor in a theatrical troupe which presented classics throughout South America. The company broke up in Venezuela where most of its members remained. In 1933 Tarranco appeared in Honrubias del Valle in the Province of Guadalajara, and was a sacristan. In the archives of the political party, Acción Popular, there is a document accusing this sacristan of Marxist activities. During the Civil War he became a captain in the Loyalist Army and distinguished himself for bravery. When Barcelona was taken by the Nationals he fled to France with some of his soldiers, and was suffering from a serious cerebral disturbance caused by a mine explosion.

No more is known of him until October 27, 1939, on which date his name was registered at the Insane Asylum in Montfort, a small French town in the Department of Ariège on the northern slopes of the Pyrenees. When rumor came that the Germans were coming in that direction the patients were turned loose and the staff fled.

Morales is certain that this actor-sacristan-soldier is none other than Captain Contreras. Tarranco, attracted by the remoteness of the terrain, may well have crossed the French-Spanish border over the mountains and sought refuge in the gamewarden's hut. Logically, Salvador Yuste, being a doctor and realizing the refugee's mental illness, would have treated him. Was that perhaps when the doctor, moved by the lure of a fame he had never been able to achieve, conceived the idea of "resuscitating" him, making him believe that he was a survivor of another century? Since as a municipal doctor he had contacts with the reporters who would ask him for news, would he not have informed Antonio Cornejo of the arrival of the refugee with amnesia? Would not Cornejo have then proposed to the doctor the meticulous preparation for their hoax, letting the man grow his beard and nails until it was time for the big coup of springing his pretended disinterment on the world?

Morales cites the following excerpts from the text as worthy of attention:

"Yuste had coached the gamewarden and his daughter to give him the facts by doses, as though they were pills of thought, so that they would not upset the small mental world of the patient with the tremendous truth." And, "Everything, steps, nourishment, *ideas,* was measured . . . by the doctor." And particularly this: "When Contreras slept, Yuste spoke in his ear as though to direct his dreams, preparing Contreras' subconscious for the truth."

Morales thinks these words of Cornejo give him away. Doesn't all this, the direction of dreams, the doling out of ideas, denote a clear intention to graft a false personality on that poor victim of amnesia? Morales regrets that his attempts to find someone in France who could identify Captain Alfredo Tarranco by Contreras' photographs failed owing to the change in population during the World War and the impossibility of knowing the whereabouts of Tarranco from his first entry into France to his registration in the insane asylum. Honrubio del Valle, the village in which the man was a sacristan, was completely destroyed during the Civil War. In spite of the impossibility of proving his hypothesis for the reasons mentioned above, Morales insists that the many coincidences which accumulated around the amnesiac actor indicate that he was the resurrected Captain Contreras.

Morales goes on to discuss the discrepancy in Chapter VII of his memoirs, in which Valenzuela and Luigi, just before inducing his artificial death, ask him what is his last request, and Contreras replies: "My sword."

This sword which was supposedly placed in the famous casket next to the Captain's shrouded body was not there when the body was discovered in Almudena Cemetery.

The undeniable impression of authenticity of some of the episodes is understandable, Morales claims, since they were taken directly from *The Adventures of Captain Contreras*, the scanty memoirs of the genuine Contreras, published by the *Revista de Occidente* (and first published in 1900 by the Bulletin of the Academy of History).

Cornejo's book, often bombastic, discursive, repetitious and more concerned with form than with content, in several instances condemns its own author.

Morales finds unacceptable the change undergone by "the modern" Contreras. Morales writes: "Cornejo needed for his plans a Contreras with a critical twist, someone able to put his fingers on the foibles and weaknesses of our generation, someone able to raise storms of enthusiasm or controversy with his words. Alfredo Tarranco, or whoever played the part of Contreras, was a mediocre actor, and Cornejo, first in the newspapers then in his book, put into his mouth whatever best suited his purpose. But he didn't even do this well, for the poems, speeches and criticisms of the fake Captain just do not fit the personality of the man who wrote the actual memoirs."

In this case Morales was right. He was also right when he charged Antonio Cornejo with fraud, subornation and forgery, as the passport used by Cornejo for his trip to the United States was acquired by means of bribery, and the insurance policy on his body made out to Roosevelt University was very cleverly forged. The most serious of the charges against the reporter has not yet been proved.

In this last instance, as in his attempt to identify Contreras with Tarranco, Morales failed. There appears to have been an agreement between Yuste and Cornejo to exploit the falsification of Contreras. But it will always remain a complete mystery how Yuste or Cornejo introduced that "embalmed" body into the casket that was moved from Santo Tomé to Almudena.

Even today, so long after Cornejo's arrest, there are still people who go on believing in Contreras' miraculous survival. It's as inexplicable in itself as were many of the arguments used to deny it.

Dr. Yuste, from the insane asylum to which he was committed ("to exonerate him from criminal responsibility," as the colleague who declared him insane confesses), shouted to anyone who would listen that the man found in Almudena Cemetery was the same Contreras who lived in the seventeenth century. Yuste shouted till he was hoarse that his one mistake was in having prematurely asserted by sheer instinct that it was true, without waiting for the scientific proof. But, he raved, the evidence had finally appeared to vindicate his many hours of work and investigation, and he was willing to demonstrate it any time.

He shouted that he was a pioneer of science and that if the world put him away the way they did Miguel Servet, discoverer of the circulation of the blood, it was because present-day society was a process of decay and didn't deserve him.

One day his protests, his pleadings and his threats were heard no more.

"You've murdered him," remarked Cornejo from his jail cell when he knew that Yuste was dead. "He's a martyr who will one day make you stand up and admit the truth for which he lived and died: the resurrected man of Almudena *was* Captain Contreras! What can I say to prove it to you? The whole thing is true, true!"

During the first stage of the proceedings against Cornejo (a trial which is still dragging on with respect to the more serious charge) some people who had been closest to the Captain were called as witnesses. The Countess of Alcedo, who failed to win her suit for libel against Cornejo, had come from Oslo where, seven months after the Captain's last act, she had established residence.

"Antonio Cornejo," Paca Revilla declared, "is too little a person to have created the sublime character that was Captain Contreras. It's impossible for a creator to be inferior to his creation. Cornejo didn't have the stature to be Contreras' bootblack let alone his creator."

"Cornejo," declared Don José "Pepe" Castejón, Marqués del Darro, "was literarily without taste. Read, for example, his description of a dawn in Chapter Twelve, or his descriptions of just about anything for that matter — tasteless and pedestrian. I agree completely with the Countess of Alcedo: Whoever knew Captain Contreras well cannot conceive that this man was a product of Señor Cornejo. Captain Contreras, gentlemen, was a real, a serious and an important person. May I be permitted to suggest that there are still many points to be cleared up in this trial, among them the question of the personality of the man who, according to Inspector Morales, passed himself off as Captain Contreras. It's absolutely inconceivable that this actor Tarranco was the same man whom we knew."

"Would the Marqués del Darro care to explain why not?"

"Because with an actor of that quality," shouted Castejón, "the company he belonged to wouldn't have fallen apart in Venezuela!"

(Laughter.)

"Then does the witness suggest that Señor Cornejo's straw man was really Captain Contreras?"

"Sir, it is the simplest explanation, it is the only explanation."

"My lord, pardon the witness," interrupted the Prosecutor sarcastically. "We must remember that the Marqués del Darro is a poet."

Among the witnesses was a certain beautiful novitiate from the Convent of the Adorers of the Sacred Heart. Since her Superior forbade her to make a declaration, the Court had to obtain a special dispensation from the

Bishop. Because of the particular circumstances and past of the witness the Court agreed to take her testimony behind closed doors — and without disclosing her name.

To summarize: Of the many charges which fell on Cornejo's shoulders the only ones which were tried at that time were bribery and forgery. The most serious charge has still to be aired, hence the interest of this publishing house in printing the book while it may still be of benefit to the author.

Putting it briefly, and of course inconclusively, since this case has dragged on and on and has not yet shown signs of ending, Cornejo was charged with murdering his creation, Contreras, when the latter refused to go through with the lucrative lecture Cornejo had planned. The newspaperman struck the Captain viciously from behind, it is charged, the night before that lecture was to have taken place. The victim then somehow made his way to his orchard home, where he succumbed much in the manner described in the accused's book. Lack of evidence, witnesses, and the whole unreal aura about the case has hampered and protracted the trial.

We insist that we cannot bring ourselves to believe in the truth of the Contreras case, any more than we can explain it; even so, this work will be an invaluable document for following the course of Spain's most fantastic and as yet unexplained event of the century; for Antonio Cornejo is right in this: the case must represent the most extraordinary case of mass autosuggestion on record, if that's what it is.

We at this publishing house are about to embark upon

a full-scale investigation of the Roosevelt University studies made on Contreras, and our findings and report will quite possibly make a revealing book in itself at some future date.

But perhaps the most exceptional thing is that no matter what the conclusions of that book are, no matter what the outcome of the trial, no matter what is said in articles or books like this, a great many people will continue to believe that a man named Contreras had not just one life — but two.